Wise's first collection of short stories, the award-winning *Night Train, Cold Beer,* was blunt, honest, cinematic. This collection, *Resume Speed*, is also visually keen, and each story gives you the impression of having entered a town where, though the city limit sign welcomes you, something is amiss. As each story ends, you punch the accelerator to get to the next. From noir to ironic, flash fiction to longer form, *Resume Speed* is an odyssey of exceptional storytelling. "I'll just give you a warning this time. Have a nice day," as the cop behind the mirrored sunglasses might say.

ACKNOWLEDGEMENTS

A shorter version of *Argo and the Sirens*, titled *The Sirens of Lake Texoma*, appeared in *Flyover Country*, and the *Resume Speed* version appeared in *Thrice Fiction Magazine*. *A Night at the Jubilee Room* appeared in *Dying Goose*. *Speaking French in Kurtz Territory* appeared in *Atticus*. *Strong the Pink* appeared in *Santa Fe Writers Project*. *Exhuming Captain Midnight* appeared in *Amarillo Bay*. *Desert Dog* appeared in *Commuter Lit*. *What Wade Clover Did in 1958* appeared in *Prick of the Spindle*. *Hardball* (of *Ten Circumstances*) appeared in *Gravel*. *Blue Moon, High Bridge,* and *Transgression* (of *Ten Circumstances*) appeared in *Randomly Accessed Poetics*. *The Hole in the Ceiling at the Refuge Tavern* was anthologized in *Best New Writing*, 2015. *Wing Walker* appeared in *Cactus Heart Review*. *Midnight Robot* appeared in *Dirty Chai*. *Jesus Rust* appeared in *Blacktop Passages*. *Train Time* appeared in *Work Literary Magazine*. *The Woman Who Looked Like Lana Turner* appeared in *Switchback Review*. *Old Ordnance* and *The Performance* both appeared in *Hypertext Magazine*. *John Settle* appeared in *Shotgun Honey*.

RESUME SPEED

STORIES BY
GUINOTTE WISE

A Black Opal Books Publication

RESUME SPEED ~ STORIES BY GUINOTTE WISE
Copyright © 2016 by Guinotte Wise
Cover Design by Ben Carmean
All cover art copyright © 2016
All Rights Reserved
Print ISBN: 978-1-626944-84-8

First Publication: JUNE 2016

Published by Black Opal Books **http://www.blackopalbooks.com**

*For Tim, who read most of these
and whose comments are taken to heart.
Get well. I'm writing more.*

Table of Contents

ARGO AND THE SIRENS

In June of 1955, on a humid Thursday, Brad East-wood walked over to Elmer Apple's table at The Sportsman Cafe in Madill, Oklahoma, his hard hat in his hand.

"Mr. Apple?"

"Elmer. Mr. Apple's six foot under and good for him."

"Elmer." Brad introduced himself. "Me and my friend got shit-canned over at Worthington for not putting up with the foreman, Curry, anymore, and—"

"What form did this not putting up with him take?"

"Form. Oh. I knocked him asshole over teakettle off the bank and into Lake Texoma. Shallow enough where he landed but he was wet. Angry."

"Why did you do that?"

"He come at me after he called my friend George a nigger and I told him to shut up or put up."

Elmer wiped his mouth with a napkin and turned in his chair to face Brad. Elmer's expression was earnest and he gave Brad his full attention. "Why did he call your friend a nigger?"

"Well—" Brad smiled slightly. "—he told George to hurry up and George says 'I only got two speeds and if you don't like this one, I know you ain't gonna like the other one.'"

Elmer laughed. "What can I do for you?"

"I was wondering if you had any spots open on your core-drilling rig."

"For George of the two speeds, and you of the ready fists."

"Right."

"I'll try you both out. Be at the low cutbank on the Oklahoma side at 7:30. I'll pick you up in the *Lone Star* then."

ॐॐ

Elmer ran Tulsa Testers, a core-drilling outfit, and technically, he worked for Worthington Construction, so Brad and George would, *technically*, be working for their previous employer.

The barge was fifty by forty with two rigs on it, each with Mission mud pumps, and they drilled into the basin of Lake Texoma from the barge, bringing up cylindrical sample after sample from various depths in the rock. The lake was about 100 feet deep in the middle. On the sides of the barge was stenciled, white paint mingling with the rust, *ARGO*. It was named for the ship that Jason sailed after the golden fleece in Greek mythology, Elmer told them, as he often drilled for black gold when not in testing mode. Elmer called those who worked on his barge, Argonauts. "When people ask what it means, you can tell them that, or the more common answer," he said with a laugh.

The barge was moved every week and secured by thick cables at all corners to concrete "dead men." The lake itself was a mile across where the bridge was being built from the Oklahoma side to Texas, and the core testing would last several months before they moved on. Maybe Brad and George would do well enough to move with Tulsa Testers. Elmer told them he'd make roughnecks of them if they were willing workers, that it was just like the oil patch, the testing work, and though it was a hard dollar it was a glorious dollar.

The next morning they were ready, with their thermoses and lunchboxes. Elmer waved from the *ARGO* far out in the lake, and they could see him starting the outboard on the little aluminum boat tied to the side of the barge, the sun flashing on his driller's hard hat. The hat looked old fashioned compared to the short-billed hard hats George and Brad wore, like a WWI helmet, only aluminum. Brad thought maybe they'd get to wear driller's hats if they did well enough, proved themselves.

c凶c凶

They carried pipe from a neat pile and threaded sections in place, one after another, chain-wrench tightened it, then another. This went on until noon, at which time they broke for lunch under the shade of a canvas sheet on a box frame, open at the sides to the breeze. The barge was constantly moving, it seemed at first, but now they were used to it, their centers having picked up the nuances of the lake's various moods.

"George," said Elmer.

George looked up from his thick ham and egg on white, smiled.

"Your speed is fine."

George and Brad laughed. Elmer made a fist at Brad, and they laughed again.

c凶c凶

After lunch, they downed cups of water at the Igloo and Elmer pointed out the container of salt tablets. Elmer went to measure diesel fuel. Brad noticed the men on the Texas side moving toward the reinforcing steel they were tying, and used Elmer's binoculars for a closer look. Curry was standing off from the men eying the barge, fists on his hips, legs spread.

"C'mere," Brad said to George. He pointed out Curry, then started doing a tap dance, with his hand in a salute at his forehead. George joined him. Curry could see their crazy silhouettes dancing. He turned and strode off.

Elmer said, "Boys, I think there's a no-shit storm brewing over west."

They looked. A dirty gray curtain of clouds and rain was forming an anvil about a mile away. They rushed to chain down the loose pipe, tie down whatever would roll or be lost from the barge in rough water. By the time they finished, it was too late to get to shore in the *Lone Star*, the waves swamping it.

"Sorry, boys, we can only tie ourselves to the rigs, now. Hope for the best," Elmer yelled above the rain.

He helped Brad tie George, then he tied Brad next to him, leaving their arms free so they could get loose when the time came. Then Elmer slipped and slid to the other rig. The barge was shifting and yawing up and down with the waves. The temperature had dropped at least twenty degrees, maybe thirty.

A mountainous presence lurched and groaned toward them with a roar like a freight train only louder. "Tornado," yelled Brad, but George couldn't hear him. They were tied at ninety-degree corners on the derrick facing away from one another and the wind snapped their shirts, stinging their faces with the collars.

Brad's hardhat blew off, clanged against the derrick and skittered like a live thing up and off into the dark chaos. The wind and rain hurt now, whipped and manhandled him like a mad drunken daddy. The floor of the barge took an impossible angle to the water, then slammed back down, and the waves leaped over their heads. He couldn't see Elmer, some twenty feet away, then an instant of relative clarity, lightning maybe, showed a long two-by-four hit the rig to which Elmer was lashed, about ten feet up, spin around it, and it was gone. It had to have come all the way from the Texas bank.

Brad felt the plate steel beneath his feet shudder and pound like something alive was under the barge and clawing to come up through it. When the hail started, it was almost orchestral, kettledrums, snares, poppity-pop and boom and click against the deck, depending on the size of the pellets hitting the resounding steel plate.

He cocked his head as the keening sound began. His first thought was the cables: they were stretched to breaking in the slate-gray frothing violence. And they did make a zinging sound when they yanked against the dead men deep on the lake floor. But this was different. It sounded like the middle notes of a pack of coyotes howling, but sweeter, less throaty yet more powerful. He recognized it as singing. It sounded like a hundred Patsy Clines and The Chordettes and The McGuire Sisters, all at once, yet it was like nothing he'd heard in his twenty-two years of living. It promised him calm, safety, loving arms, a continual crescendo of sexual reward, and more, if only he'd free himself from earthly ropes and bonds and slip out of the tempest's roar and churn, slide down into the tranquility of the voices' lair, just beneath the turbulent waves of

Lake Texoma. Down there, the voices told him, they'd take over. "Leave your hard life behind," they sang, "we'll take you down the Red River in freshets to the sea where life began and where you'll begin. Down the Atchafalaya to the gulf, the warm gulf waters, where we'll play and love and sing with whales."

He believed it. He had a dim knowledge of the Red River, but had not known it connected with the Atchafalaya, and emptied into the gulf.

At that point a hail ball the size of a cantaloupe hit the derrick and his head, the steel taking most of the impact, yet he was knocked unconscious, head down on his chest, shirt torn away from his bleeding shoulders by the razor wind. The racket intensified, the flotsam blowing through contained parts of the Worthington tugboat in which Curry and his crew had tried to reach the Oklahoma side, and almost had, until the boat was lifted into the air, twin diesels screaming with the sudden freedom from water resistance, the screws flashing.

A dead chicken flew through at eye level. A Zippo lighter slid across the steel deck, spun and stopped at the chained pipe pile where it chattered and jumped like a big chrome bug. Branches and vines carried from Texas whirled up into the howling gritty vortex, but the Zippo stayed, dancing in place.

George remained conscious during all this and the voices that beckoned to him sounded like Mahalia Jackson, The Shirelles, and The Supremes, among others, but not exactly if he had to describe the sound. Maybe a choir. But not right. Much more suggestive, although the choir singing he'd heard in church had made his mind wander under the robes. They, the voices, wanted him to be un-hindered, even reckless—fear no man, no thing, no fiery crosses, and follow them into the lake, the depths, the kingdom come, and the slick bodies and the moaning pleasures thereof. Temptation. Release. An underworld of smoky saxophone, lubricious grinding, slowly tangled limbs, and no burnt aftertaste of shame, only wonders upon wonders, each better than the last. Could it be?

George couldn't swim, was afraid of water, yet he struggled with the wet knots and cursed the ropes that bound him to the derrick, cursed those who'd tied the knots. He wanted his forevers to be with the voices. They wanted him as much as he wanted them, damn Elmer and Brad tying him like this. The knots were water-soaked, swollen tight. The voices, the forever, was leaving him to suffer on earth. He stamped his feet in frustration and yearning, the thick-soled workboots thumping the plate steel beneath him.

Brad heard the stamping and cursing from a groggy distance, although George was quite near him. He mean-dered in and out of consciousness, licking blood that came to his lips from his forehead. He wiped his face with his wet hands, looked at the blood on them, thought head wounds bled a lot, but he seemed to be okay other-wise. He was only then aware that the swirling dirty mass of water and sand and clanging things had left them and was chasing itself east on the lake with waterspouts and evil bursts of greenish light, its wall a revolving terror of rain, brush, and writhing shapes.

He looked over his right shoulder to the water near the barge. It wasn't calm, still white and choppy, but nothing like it had been. The barge was yawing on its cables, but all four had held. A dim memory, like a half evaporated dream, voices, promising. What was that? He attributed it to the knock on the head. His shirt had been torn off in the melee, strips of the denim remained under the ropes. He rested his head back on the derrick and let the swaying motion of the barge take over, not fighting for equilibrium, letting the ropes hold him.

The sun poked shafts through the clouds and rippling pools on the deck of the barge reflected into Brad's eyes. The Zippo winked at him from the chained stack of pipe.

Elmer's voice came from nearby. "The devil's beating his wife, boys. And we are three lucky sumbitches." He cut through George's ropes with a small pocketknife.

"Why wasn't you here earlier?" said George.

Elmer said, as he freed him, "And if thou shalt implore and bid thy comrades to loose thee, then let them bind thee with yet more bonds." Then he started on Brad's ropes. "Man you got socked pretty good by something, How do you feel?"

"I feel okay," said Brad. "Maybe kind of like I'm gonna puke, though."

"I tied myself facing into the storm like a fool. Got hit in the chest by a bird going about ninety, felt like a concrete football. We'll get us back to the Oklahoma side if that *Lone Star* is still there. You'll have to row, though. I think my ribs are cracked."

George stood at the edge of the barge, looking into the choppy water with a vacant stare. Then he helped Brad tug on the chain to the sunken *Lone Star*. They managed to get a winch cable to one of the oarlocks, pull it slowly to the deck, turn it keel up.

"I had a dream," said George. "Voices like a beautiful choir, like more than that, promising things…" His voice trailed off and he made gestures to show how fruitless it was to try to explain.

"I think I might have, too," said Brad. He looked into the water.

"It's the water sireens," said Elmer. "Help me get this motor off."

George poured water from a tray of box-end wrenches from the chain-link cage and began to loosen bolts, saying to Elmer, "You sit down. Broke ribs can stick your lung. We'll get this."

"The water sireens?" said Brad.

"The death angels. When you're on bodies of water long enough, big ones, you'll hear 'em during certain kinds of storms," said Elmer. "I don't want to say too much because they're listening. They're still here, I can feel them. But a wall of water half from the sky and half from the lake or ocean or wherever summons them up. They sing through your head is the best I can explain it. They use what you know and think about and dream up, and promise it to you in spades."

"So they're in your head," said George.

"I didn't say that. They *use* what's in your head. It's irresistible, what we fantasize. All the voices do is pry it loose. Amplify it. Feed it back to you."

"They're real?" asked Brad.

"I didn't say that either. It's a phenomenon. It's...evil concentrated, whirled, whipped up." He shook his head. "Hard to explain."

"Jesus!" said George, and he backed away from the *Lone Star*, eyes wide.

Brad looked, and the hair on his neck rose. It was a body, bumping along the side of the barge with what looked like a Ku Klux Klan hood on his head. But the hood was just a trick of vision. It was a shirt pulled up over his head with holes in it. He was face down in the water, arms spread out Christ-like, the shirt floating to a wavering hood-looking point above the shoulders.

When they'd wrestled the sodden body onto the deck, they turned it over on the now steaming steel plate.

"It's Curry," said Brad.

George said nothing, his face impassive, head down, eyes hidden in shadow.

"One speed, now," Brad said. "Sorry, didn't mean to speak ill of the dead."

And he began laughing, trying not to. George looked at him, thought of their little dance before the storm, and he began laughing too. Elmer watched them, quizzically. Their hysteria wore down and the laughter sputtered.

"There might be more out there, boys," Elmer said. "I know you're not laughing because it's funny…"

"No sir," George said. "Nothing funny about any of this. I just can't help it."

"I know. We'll all be fine in time. We've been through quite a lot."

The Army Corps of Engineers sent a boat out to the barge to pick them up. Another boat was sent for Curry's body. Brad had picked up the Zippo lighter and stuck it in his jeans pocket. On the way back to the Oklahoma side, he remembered it, took it out to look at it. The Army Corps guy was a speed demon, the small boat jarring Brad's teeth as it hit each choppy little wave, making it hard to see the inscription on the lighter.

It was inscribed UKA, which he knew to be United Klans of America. It was probably Curry's. In any case, it was bad luck, evil, like the storm that blew it to them. He let the hand holding it trail in the water, released it, turned to watch its silvery shape descend.

One thing sure, thought Brad, he would never get caught in a storm on water again if he could help it.

A NIGHT AT THE JUBILEE ROOM

It was the late nineteen-fifties. Cold War, boom times, mixed ebullience, and dread were served up in fairly equal amounts. The same can be said of most eras, I guess. The difference was, I was young, full of hormones and optimism, and a rebellious nature that dismissed all the admonishments about "starving artists" and getting a certain kind of higher education so I could land a "real job," an adult job. I'd spent three years at two other colleges and made a break for the Art Institute in my home town of Kansas City. I felt like I'd been sprung from prison. This was the life. Paint and draw and drink. Holler on the street corners. Cut loose. I ran with a group of shaggy rebels and the girls were not only free with sex, some demanded it. I was where I was supposed to be, was the overwhelming feeling I had about it.

But I had no money, so I worked various jobs to make ends meet. I worked in the campus cafeteria, at a

Philipp's 66 station, then I got a night job in a mortuary. I was on duty there from six to ten at night, ushering the bereaved into staterooms, as they called them, to see their favorite dead people. Then from ten on, I was free to study or sleep or roam the place all night until six in the morning. So, six to six, twelve hours in a mortuary. Thing is I had to have a "decent" haircut, and wear a suit. People would die in the early morning hours and off we'd go, me and Verne, to pick them up, bring them back for draining, prep, etc. I didn't do any of the latter, of course. Nor did I watch any of it. That was just too strange to consider. Nights could be, as you can imagine, kind of depressing without getting into the formaldehyde and suture aspects.

There were lighter moments, like the night manager, Bill Hanrahan, helping us lift someone from the gurney, and change falling out of the dead guy's pockets. "Lunch money," he'd shout, but he'd put it in a manila envelope, with rings, watches, keys, whatever. Then he'd ask me what size shoe I wore, and I'd tell him, and he'd look at the guy's shoes and say, "Too bad, too small. Alligator, too," or something like that.

He had a spiel he'd do when a bigwig would occupy the stainless steel draining table. He'd say "This old boy was a big power in the newspaper business, but now he's on the great leveling table." He'd put his palms together, then spread his arms wide, indicating the table and the person, and he'd say it theatrically, like an old time preacher, with his lips all pursed and he'd draw out the word "great" as he spread his arms. "Now he's where we'll all be some day, no richer, no poorer than any of us. The greeeaaaat leveling table. Yessir."

Sermon over, Verne would open up his Wall Street Journal to check his stocks while the night crew would start laying out their tools. And I'd leave to study, sleep, or roam the halls of the quiet, elegant old building.

I'd take the phone some nights. Bill's girlfriend called and thought I was him, said she wanted some information on burying a stiff. I was speechless. She said, "You say how long is this stiff? And I say about eight inches," and she brayed like a donkey, I swear.

Made me laugh. Or some giggling girl would call and say "I'm dying to meet you," and hang up amidst her slumber partying friends' shrieks.

You'd think a mortuary would be spooky at night, but it wasn't. The halls were tastefully lit and full of good paintings. Seascapes and landscapes. Early California expressionists. They had some money tied up in art.

I'd get a clean dead-sheet from the linen supply, take off my suit and hang it carefully, wrap up in the sheet, and sleep on one of the comfortable couches in an empty stateroom. If I was lucky, I'd sleep clear through to six, dress in my school clothes, and head to class. Sometimes, though, Verne would wake me at some small hour and tell me to get dressed, dead people alert. I was Verne's assistant. He was a night man by choice.

Off we'd go to a hospital, old folks home, or private residence where the death certificate had been signed by a doctor. I'd drive, Verne would sleep. We always used a Plymouth wagon, black like the Cadillac hearses, and with a small mortuary name in the side windows. The side windows had screen-like panels in them but you could still see in. There was a track on the back floor that would accept the gurney wheels and then you could lock it in place so it wouldn't roll it around. We'd strap the body in, check the covering sheet, lock it in. Anyway, that's where Verne would sleep on the way over to pick up a deceased. He'd lay on the gurney, hands folded on his chest until I'd get to the address.

One night about three a.m., we pulled up to a stoplight, him in back, on view through the side windows, and a carload of girls pulled alongside. They started hollering at me, they were obviously enjoying a night of partying, and I looked over.

"How are things at the mortuary?" one yelled.

"Kinda dead," I said.

They all laughed and then Verne sat up, wondering what all the noise was. They hauled ass, the driver lost control of the car and hopped a curb, bumped into a traffic light. Not our problem, said Verne, so I drove off when the light changed.

One evening we had to pick up a body at a party. Nice house in Leawood, a fashionable suburb of KC. Two brothers lived there, both doctors, one had passed away during the party. That didn't stop the festivities. We had to say "Pardon me" about ten times just to get the gurney past knots of guests who were talking, laughing. The bar area was the worst, just getting through the people who didn't want to give up their place near the booze where a Black bartender was busy making and pouring drinks. He smiled sadly at me, as I asked people to move, shook his head almost imperceptibly. I smiled back, rolled my eyes, and he winked. The dead doc was in a back bedroom, on a bed with a bunch of coats and hats. I looked at Verne, but he'd seen it all, had no expression.

Verne flapped out a crisp, knife-edge folded sheet, laid it on the gurney. We adjusted the scissor legs of the gurney down to bed height, rolled the doc onto it, pulled the sheet over him head to toe, strapped him in, rolled back out through the noisy party. It was about eight o'clock at night, shame to shut the party down so early. I guess that was their rationale. His brother followed us out to the wagon, drink in hand.

"We were expecting it, actually," he said.

"So you had a party," I wanted to say, but didn't.

"Bad ticker." He patted his chest with his free hand. "Mine isn't the best. We might see you boys again soon."

Verne muttered to me, "Two-for-one special, Doc. Hurry it up, though."

I snorted, turned it into a cough. "Well, sure sorry, Doctor."

He looked over his shoulder at the house. "I'd better

be getting back. You have the papers, right?"

I reached into my suit breast pocket, pulled them out, put them under one of the straps holding the sheeted body.

"Bye, brud," he said, lifting his drink in the deceased's direction. "He'd want it this way," he said to me, smiled, and turned, walked back up the sidewalk.

"Fuck's sake," Verne said, chuckling.

We hefted the folded-down gurney into the wagon, locked it in place.

That night we had another one, at a hospital. An older woman died, maybe seventy. We had to pick her up and carry her to the gurney this time, the way her bed was situated and all the monitors around it. I had her shoulders. Her head fell back toward me and she made a harsh gasping sound.

I almost dropped her. "Verne, she's alive!"

Verne explained that dead people often made noises due to trapped air in their systems, that, sadly, no she was not alive. He said he'd seen people move in the prep room, maybe their arm would go up and fall back on the stainless steel table, once in a great while someone would sit up. Another solid reason for me to stay out of there, I felt.

I disliked wearing a suit and tie every night after classes, and my one good blue suit was getting shiny at the elbows and knees. I started looking for a different job. It wasn't just the suit thing that got to me, it was like a quick succession of things. One night when I couldn't sleep, I was outside the mortuary, a Spanish style building, having a smoke, even though back then you could smoke inside just about anywhere. I noticed a roil of black smoke coming from a chimney on a separate building that Verne had identified as the crematorium. Someone was being reduced to ashes and it bummed me out. The smoke obliterated the stars near rooftop, then became a part of the night sky.

I flipped the cigarette butt into the parking lot and looked at the stars. It wasn't the first time I'd looked at the cold stars in the vast sky and thought about how insignificant we all were. Then, that night, Bill, the night manager, woke me up. "Get ready for a long night, plane crash landing at the airport."

Verne was pulling body bags from some storage facility and I was wondering what the hell I would do at such a scene. Turned out the plane belly-landed okay in foam, and everyone was safe. I couldn't shake the scene in my mind, though, after all the talk of other nights not so fortunate.

Then, about eight o'clock one night, a friend of my folks' was wheeled in. A woman I knew, who'd choked on a piece of steak at a restaurant. Dead. I recalled how lively she'd been, pretty and fun. I went to the prep room to make sure, could be someone with a similar name, and there she was, naked on a prep table. I felt like I was intruding. It was her all right, I could tell by the face and hair, but she was anything but vivacious, now; her skin tone was slightly blue. My eyes strayed to the rest of her, her breasts, stomach and pubic hair, the slight rounding of her stomach and mons. The thought that I was seeing a friend of the family naked, defenseless in death, struck me as over some line, boundary, that I'd crossed, and the information seeping through my brain—that here was an attractive woman about whom I'd once had thoughts of a sexual nature when she was alive—was so offensive I turned and walked out, feeling slightly ill.

"See a ghost?" said Verne.

I hurried past him to the greeting area, where I woodenly escorted people into various family staterooms, a new appreciation of the finality of death forming in my mind. At ten o'clock, I readied for sleep, as usual, but finally got up, dressed in my morning school clothes, and walked around the mortuary, looking closely at the oil paintings, the brushstrokes. I tried to read my notes for a test coming up, but my mind wandered.

I reflected on death. I was twenty-one, had bounced around in college, gone to two universities, and now the Art Institute, aimless in a way, but embraced college, figured if I worked I could just keep going, spend my life in college. It wasn't as expensive back then, and there were scholarships and hardship grants. Seemed a decent way to live, at least for a while.

But now, death was a constant thought. I'd seen death before, even though I hadn't been in the military. And Vietnam was looming. I needed to get away from the mortuary—it was corrosive somehow. It brought the specters too close. I wasn't cut out for this, even as a temporary situation. I decided to make it more temporary and gave notice.

Back at school, I put the word out, looking for a job that would allow me to attend classes during the day, an evening job would be best. I checked the bulletin board, considered being a vet's assistant over on Main Street, a clinic I'd seen. It was daytime and weekends. But that had to do with sickness, pain. I kept looking.

I stopped in at Dave's Stagecoach Inn for a beer. Several of us had done a mural on his walls in the pool-room—Dave was art institute-friendly. I asked Dave if he knew of any part time jobs that would fit hours such as mine.

"You free evenings?" he asked.

He told me to check with Mike at The Jubilee Room over on Main. I was familiar with it, had dropped in a couple of times. It was an older person's place, a sports bar, in that boxers and reporters hung out there. Kind of a dive, but a cool dive if you know what I mean. Fedoras, loosened ties, some working stiffs, construction guys in their coveralls, not many women. I knew who Mike was—ex-fighter, tough-looking guy with a worked-over face, cauliflower ears, beefy, gray hair in a bristly crew cut, looked like a movie convict. White shirt, sleeves pushed up, bar apron, he'd take drinks and beers to tables and booths, pick up something that looked like close enough payment, sometimes more, sometimes less, say in a WC Fieldsian drawl, "Whatever's fair…" But it always seemed to work out.

I sat on a barstool at the end where I might catch him for few minutes in a semi-private conversation.

"Hi, uhh, Mike?"

"You old enough to drink, kid?" He squinted at me from the other end of the bar while scraping the suds off the top of two draws with a wooden ruler-looking thing.

"Sure. Been here before."

"Were you old enough then?"

"Yessir, I was," I said.

"What can I get you?"

"Well, I heard from Dave that you had a night job available, bartender, I…"

He set the two beers down in front of me, said, "The two gents in the booth by the window, hats hanging on the clothes hook. They run a tab."

I picked up the draws by the handles, felt somewhat unsteady and out of place moving around the tables, set the beers down on their booth table, and picked up their empties. They continued talking and merely nodded at me.

I returned to the end of the bar, and Mike handed me a tray with a bottle of Schlitz, a glass, and what looked like two bourbons on the rocks. "Table by the shuffle-board. Get three dollars and forty cents. They'll tell you who gets what drink."

I came back with a five and Mike made change. "Cheap bastids didn't tell ya to keep it, eh?" He slid the change at me. I dropped it off at the table where three questionable-looking guys stopped talking as I did so. Probably planning a bank robbery, I thought.

"Get back here and make what I tell ya," Mike said, motioning with his head to behind the bar. I stepped up a couple of inches on some slatted flooring, again, feeling conspicuous, though a bit taller. I assumed the rails were for spilled beverages but they seemed odd to walk on.

"Two draws, two shots, a scotch and water."

I looked around for the mugs, found them, started filling one.

"Slower. You'll get all suds that way. Tilt the mug some." He sort of drawled everything out of the corner of his mouth in a forced higher register and, if he was imitating WC Fields, he was doing a damn good job of it. I chortled appreciatively.

"Somethin' funny, kid?"

"Uh, no, sir," I said, immediately realizing this was just the way he talked naturally. "I'm just wondering what I'm doing."

"Well, if you don't know, how the fuck you gonna be my night guy?"

I grabbed two shot glasses and reached for a bottle of bourbon. He stopped my arm. "When they just say shot, use this." He pulled a bottle of Colonel Lee, handed it to me.

It had a pour cork in it, I glugged two pretty healthy shots, but not too full to carry.

Mike nodded, approvingly. "Now when they name a whiskey, this here's a list for cost. Most everything's the same except for Chivas and Wild Turkey. It ain't rocket science, and it ain't art school." Then he added, "Mitch."

"How'd you—"

"I never forget a face, a name, or how someone acts. You was polite to my ol' lady when she was helping out one night. Shitty tipper, but hey, you're a student."

I hadn't been in there for months, hardly remembered that time the woman waited on us, but vaguely formed a picture of her in my mind. She'd been harried, not particularly memorable. "How is your wife?"

"Shot in a holdup."

"Oh, shit! I—I'm sorry—"

"Her own damn fault. She held up a federal marshal, fucker was armed. Doing five to twenty for that."

I couldn't speak.

He said, "Scotch and water, c'mon, c'mon." He pointed to a lower-priced Scotch. I poured, looked for a tap. He touched a pair of chrome knobs, said "Always use this for water, this for soda. They want Coke or 7-Up or whatever, use the bottles."

"Who gets this?"

"End of the bar. Beer and Scotch first. Come back and get the shots. Those three clowns in suits. I was kidding about the ol' lady. She's fine."

I brought a ten-dollar bill back. Mike showed me how to open the cash register for a sale, counted out the change. I laid it on the bar nearest the guy who'd paid and he slid a dollar bill at me.

"Thanks," I said, took it to Mike, who told me to stick it in my pocket.

It went like that the rest of the night. Mixed drinks, cocktails, beers, and shots, nothing fancy. I made change from the register. It was a fairly busy night so I didn't have much time to worry about how I was doing, I was just doing.

During a lull, he showed me where a sap was under the bar, and a sawed off shotgun, shells. He said, "Never use these. They're here for moral support only."

"You ever use them?"

"Once or twice. Hell ain't half full, but it got a little more crowded couple years back."

"Would you tell me about it?"

"Nope. Talkin' about that shit is bad luck." He began pulling glasses out of the soapy water, rinsing them and turning them upside down on the grated drain area after holding them to the light. "Never leave soap bubbles on glasses and mugs. Keep a pot of coffee going until closing time. Some guys like Irish Coffee, some cops come in just for coffee."

He poured the burnt old coffee out, made a fresh pot.

"That shotgun?" he said. "Most of the time we got customers who carry a piece, couple PIs, plainclothes cops, a connected guy or two. They like us and there's no use goin' for that scatter gun. They'll take care of you, anything comes up. And that's why nothin' ever comes up. Only a fool would try to rob this place. But then there's a lot of dumb fucks out there. You're in here alone? Someone comes in who's hinky? Step on this." He pointed with his foot to a large button on the floor by the cash register.

"Empty the drawer of ones, fives, tens, give it to 'em. The hundreds and most of the twenties go here, as they mount up." He dropped a twenty-dollar bill in a slot by the register, opened a door beneath it showing a combination safe.

"You don't know the combination. Lock doesn't work. Door pulls open any time."

I had to assume that he knew all about me from Dave who also knew my folks and probably vouched for my character and any virtues. Mike was not a careless sort. And this first night trial by fire was the best way to see what I was about. It worked, and the night flew by to when he clicked the house lights twice for last call. Another half hour and I'd be heading back to my rented room and blessed sleep. No classes until ten. If this job paid anything, it was perfect.

He gave me a twenty, said I had the job at more than the mortuary paid, and the tips I got, so I was euphoric. It seemed like a busy fun job and the time went fast. I could study at slow times. Maybe sketch the customers.

I worked with Mike a couple of nights until he felt comfortable leaving me on my own, but he only did that on slow nights. He was always there on weekends and Wednesday, which was a heavier night for some reason. Hump day, he called it. On a Monday, when I was alone, a gent and a lady dropped in. She was well dressed, attractive, wore green, a redhead. The guy had on a suit and tie and fedora, pocket handkerchief. He looked a little like a hood. Cold eyes. I think they were slumming and he had hoped to come upon some fighter or someone he may have known.

At any rate, she said she'd have a sidecar. He had a cocktail, easy enough, but I had to go to the Mr. Boston drink book for hers. I'd heard of a sidecar but didn't know the ingredients, and told them so, but also told them to bear with me. I made the drink, even to the fine point of dusting the wet rim of the delicate glass with sugar.

She drank it, no complaints, and the guy tipped me well. She sat at the bar and twirled a bit coquettishly, happy with a buzz, or the occasion.

I think he played some Fats Waller on the jukebox. Probably lovers or having an affair, thirty-five, maybe forty. She eyed me several times, and smiled when I noticed. Even winked once.

Then The Angel came in. He stopped on his way to the bar, a bit surprised I guess that Mike wasn't there. The Norwegian Angel, a pro wrestler. I knew who he was from his framed picture on the wall among the boxers, ballplayers, and a couple of B-movie actors. He raised his chin at me as a greeting, took a stool down the bar from the couple.

He was huge. And his face was unusual, sort of pushed in in the middle, pronounced forehead and chin. When he smiled, it looked painful. Mike had told me if The Angel ever came in, give him one on the house, maybe two if I felt like it, but at least one. He'd pointed out his signed picture to me and I'd been transfixed by the way the big man looked. Mike had said, "Gambler. In over his head with the mob, poor SOB."

The condition he had was called acromegaly and Mike said it's a bitch to live with, all kinds of side problems—headaches, vision changes, skin tissue thickening, but the main one was what they used to call gigantism, and the resulting overgrowth of various areas. The redhead called attention to one of those areas—his hands.

In a rather loud voice she said to her friend, "My god, Floyd, look at his hands!"

I found myself looking at his hands, and they were quite large, fingers like cucumbers. I looked back up at him and said, "Yessir, what'll you have?"

"Draw beer, shot of Turkey."

By that time, the redhead was next to him and her gentleman friend was standing where he had been, looking mildly amused. He lit a cigarette with an expensive-looking gold lighter, pushed his hat back on his head slightly, watching her.

"I've seen you somewhere, haven't I?" she said to The Angel.

"Could be," he said. "Movies. All bad. The ring. I wrestled for years."

"Movies. That's it! A scary one." She had hold of his right hand and was sort of caressing it, examining it.

He extricated his hand, said, to me, "Got a fifty-cent piece?"

I pulled one from the cash register and handed it to him. He took a very ornate trophy ring off one finger and held it above the bar, dropped the coin through it, smiled at her.

"Floyd, c'mere, you gotta see this," she said, excitedly to the other man. "His finger's so big, you can drop a half-dollar through his ring."

Floyd gathered up his change, left a bill on the bar, and sauntered over. The Angel looked at him, and his face changed. He lost some color or something then let out a sigh.

"It's okay, finish your drink," Floyd said.

The Angel licked his lips and looked at his hands. Then he downed the shot, took a long pull on the beer.

Floyd handed some keys to the redhead. "Go get the car. Pull it down the street about a block that way. Leave it running and stay behind the wheel. Wait for us."

I thought about the shotgun. But nothing was overtly wrong. Except Floyd was there to take The Angel away.

Two guys in a booth kept hollering "Medic!" One of

them was circling his hand in the air for another round.

Floyd looked at me. "How old are you, kid?"

"Twenty one."

"You got fifty, sixty years, you work it right. Those guys want a round. Get it." He didn't smile, he didn't frown, he looked neutral. It was all the same to him.

I nodded at the two in the booth. "Be right there," I said.

I didn't push the button on the floor when I walked toward them, wiping my damp hands on my half-apron. It wouldn't have done any good.

Mike had said The Angel was in over his head on a gambling debt. I guessed Floyd was there for that reason. The Angel's ring was still on the bar after he and Floyd left. I put it in the safe. He never came back for it.

SPEAKING FRENCH IN KURTZ TERRITORY

Summer nights on the Marais des Cygne were like I imagine the Amazon to be, deep in Kurtz territory. For no really good reason we were on the inky water in a sloshing leaky johnboat with a finicky trolling motor, rocking a little or a lot, depending on what was going on. Drunks checking trot lines at midnight. That got us to pitching and rolling with unnecessary gestures and stumbling movements, cursing, laughing, trying to figure out what the hell was on the line stringers after I dropped the flashlight into the water. It stayed on as it sank, the light descending, disappearing. The spookiest part was Pete slipping overboard and silently swimming away under water. There were three of us; Cobb, Reno Pete, and me, Travis. Cobb is my uncle, Pete's younger brother, and Pete is my old man. One scary dude. Cobb

idolizes him and I'm terrified of him. I respect him, but
sort of like I respect a mean bull.

I never minded going out night fishing or checking
trotlines with just Cobb. Looked forward to it. He and I
would drink, smoke his LaCygne Green, talk about wom-
en, star formations. It was relaxing. But with the old man
along, I always, and I mean *always*, felt like it could be
my last night on earth, my last moments alive. It appeared
unshakeably in my thoughts that he would snap, kill me,
then Cobb. It would be by knife and drowning. Or by
muscle and skin, shirtless Pete, sheened with sweat,
would use some quick snaky move, and I'd get those tat-
tooed arms front and back of my neck, his big hands on
his biceps or elbows, and my windpipe flattening like a
blacksnake on the hard-top road to the St. Cyr Compound.

We were all St. Cyrs, but Pete went by different last
names. Wood. Ward. Wanz. And the people he ran
around with called him Reno Pete. I never knew the history of that and never asked. Pete is not a guy who invites
questions.

Anyway, Pete would slip overboard almost every
time out, we never knew when, just that he wasn't in the
boat anymore. It always freaked me out. It made me want
to cry, and I'm not a little kid. I could hold my own with
any badass in the bars around Linn County, even down in
KC. I felt unbalanced when he was around or had just
been there. Like a flywheel with a chunk out of it. And
nervous. Mary Ellen said it was just a pronounced fa-

ther/son rivalry, that it was as old as the Indian burial mounds visible from my bedroom window.

I lived on the compound with Cobb and my aunt Vinita, right on the Marais des Cygne wildlife refuge. Outbuildings and barns scattered around. I had a whole building all my own, a shed-roof two-story corrugated steel building that we insulated and made into a loft apartment. Slick as anything in the city. We glassed-in the whole top north side with patio glass doors we found in KC at a salvage joint. That sun was like…freedom. It blasted in there from the marsh side of a morning. Nothing out there but geese and cranes and miles of marshy land and trees. Beautiful. Fucking lump-in-the-throat amazing. Big-ass cranes took off in slow motion like overloaded C5, transports. Foxes looked for mice pretty much out in the open and one had her litter under my front stoop. I liked to watch them leap in the tall grass to get a bird's-eye view of what's in there.

The old man. If it ever came to a showdown, I would flat give up, give myself to it like to an unbeatable monster in a movie. Hope for mercy but not expect it. Funny thing is, he's never hit me. He's a killer, I'm sure of that—things said not quite out of my hearing by family. I think people like him have only two speeds. You just don't ever want to hit that switch. After my mom died, years ago, he got a little meaner if that's possible. But he was only dangerous if you pressed him, got into his face, or wronged a blood relative.

I heard the Zippo clink behind me and jumped enough to make the boat move so that I grabbed the side. I caught a glimpse of Reno Pete's face as he lit a cigarette, his eyes dead black marbles in the glare. He winked, or I thought he did.

I yelped when a hand stroked my shoulder in the dark.

"Goosey, ain't he?" Pete's voice from the corner of his mouth, pulling on the cigarette, the glow fulgent on his face then down again.

It was all I could do not to whimper. I started to reach for a beer in the cooler, but then realized I had to pee. No way I was standing up in that boat in the middle of the Marais Des Cygne and risk going overboard into that womb-warm weird-ass water. It was only weird when Pete was around. It was benign any other time.

"I gotta take a leak," I said. "Can we get over to the bank?"

No one spoke. Thank god, they didn't tell me to just piss over the side. Someone started the trolling motor, and we headed to a mud bank. I climbed out, welcoming the relative solidity of the muddy bank, slipped a little in my pull-on Converse sneakers as I moved upward to some more or less horizontal, grassy ground. The trees joined at the top over the narrow stretch of the Marais Des Cygne where we stashed some trot lines, so it was tunnel dark with only a few stars visible through the heavily laced canopy. I started to pee but experienced a stricture when I heard movement. Then I didn't hear it anymore. A rabbit, maybe a snake, something off to my right, but I still couldn't urinate. Damn. I wasn't like Cobb and Pete, natural woods creatures. I stood until a stream started, half expecting them to start hollering at me, but saw two glows in the boat—their cigarettes, heard them talking low, indistinguishable. Finally, I was relieved and zipping up when the scream came. Jesus! It was maybe 100 feet in front of me in the woods. Was it a woman? A big cat? Some fucking Hobbit-like thing that lived in the wildlife refuge, like a chupocabre? I wanted in the boat and out of there but ran into Cobb who was heading up the bank.

"Wh—what the fuck?" I said.

"Were you hollerin'?"

"Wasn't me," I said, sliding down the bank on my ass. Cobb grabbed my T-shirt and stopped my slide.

There was Pete by the boat, calm and collected. He'd bundled some greasy shop rags and wired them to a stob, lit it with his Zippo. I noted that he'd tossed the three-prong anchor into the mud bank so we wouldn't lose the little boat.

"Mind me to bring extra fucking flashlights next time," he said, "since junior here likes throwin' 'em in the water."

This was a scene out of some Huck Finn nightmare, Pete holding a torch, his hair wild, the flames throwing deep shadows on his face, making it look like a tribal mask. I'd smoked some of Cobb's powerful LaCygne Green, had some coffee and Jack Daniels—the chemistry inside me was bubbling surreal.

"It come from over that-a-way," said Cobb, pointing in the flickery light.

I followed them, rather than wait in the solid dark on the greasy bank. We skirted a thorn tree, parted some tall trash growth, and made our way into a pine-needle floor with fallen trees and old growth giants forming a pretty solid tent overhead, but with holes big enough to see some stars and moonlit clouds. Pete stopped, motioned for us to be quiet. His torch wouldn't last much longer. Pieces of shop rag floated down, gossamer as silk, showing the weave of the fabric as it disintegrated. I was fascinated by the pink floaters, when Cobb said, "There, ten o'clock," and they took off to their left.

I'd never heard Cobb say anything like that and I laughed, it was like an old war movie with pilots talking about bogeys, I mean ten o'clock would be up in the trees wouldn't it? What a weird fucking night. Both Cobb and Pete had been in Vietnam, but I bet nobody said ten o'clock there. Maybe he'd said "There, to the left," and I got it scrambled.

Cobb's pot did that to me. He grew it in the wildlife refuge, and in his pastures by the fence line, and in horseweed where the planes would never see it. He knew where every plant was. It was supposed to be number two in the world, he said, due to the peat and rot in the refuge.

It said so in a book. LaCygne Green was originally hemp in WWII.

"Hemp at ten o'clock," I said, real low, and started laughing again.

I was sort of snorting and huffing to myself in my own pot world when I heard Pete say, "Over here. Cobb, you won't believe this shit."

Then the torch died. I stopped where I was, maybe twenty feet behind them. Pete lit his Zippo and waved it over a white form on the ground. Then he cursed and flung the lighter down, due to heat I guess. All I saw in that flash was what looked like a woman on the ground, sprawled naked.

Cobb had pulled his lighter out and they located Pete's Zippo. It *was* a woman's body on the ground.

I got closer so I could hear what they were saying. "...Raleigh's wife, LeAnne, I'm pretty sure," said Pete.

"How do you know?" said Cobb.

"That tattoo on her thigh, rose with the stem coming out of her cooter," Pete said, preoccupied.

"When the hell did you ever see that?"

"Never mind. I think she's dead. Nothing we can do for her now," Pete said.

"We can't just leave her," Cobb said.

"Right. The three of us out here, drunk and stoned. Why don't we just call the sheriff as soon as we can get in cellphone range?"

"You think Raleigh killed her?"

"Could be. She was fucking around on him. Crystal whore."

"Why here? The son of a bitch, right in our back yard, damn him…"

"Or it coulda been one a those meth-heads from town. Who knows? Thing is, no matter who or what, if we report it guess who gets the hard look and the blame?"

"Shit," said Cobb.

"She's gonna come up missing," I said. "And if they find her back in here, turkey buzzards circling, like that, well, they're gonna ask us about it, anyway."

"Unless nobody ever finds her," Pete said.

"How's that happen?" I asked.

"You two go on back to the compound. I'll see you in the morning."

Cobb said, "Come on Travis," and gave my T-shirt a tug.

I followed him to the johnboat by sound and got caught up in some thorn trees. "Wait up, Cobb. I'm in this fucking thorn thicket."

I didn't hear him come back for me and I started when I felt his big hand wrap around my elbow and followed where he pulled me. The thorn trees had bit me about ten places.

On the way back, I asked, "So what's he gonna do?"

"Disappear her at first light, walk on back."

"Disappear?"

"You don't want to know the details."

Once a game warden had disappeared in the Marais des Cygne. I was pretty sure the trolling motor on the transom was state property. The story I got, years ago, was if you want someone to disappear, gut them, put thirty pounds of log chain inside them, wrap the body in pig fence and slide them in one of the deep backwaters for the carp and cats. Cobb said there were catfish in there big as a man. In a week or two, nothing would be left but pig wire, bones, and chain. It never surfaced. We had a cache of tools and wire half a mile from here.

As little as I'd seen of the white form on the ground, I felt sick at the thought of that. Someone had done her in, someone who knew the woods. Cobb said she was a meth whore, far gone, used to be hot in her day, went wrong after Raleigh started beating on her. Raleigh was a mean drunk and, by rights, ought to be the disappeared one.

⌇⌇⌇

It was the following week that we got wind of the search party. They might comb the backwoods where we'd been, on foot and horseback. Cobb was beside himself. LaCygne Green was scattered throughout that area and sure to be discovered.

"That fuck, Raleigh. I think he's behind this. Brought her in where the plants are," Cobb said.

Pete just lit a Pall Mall. "Don't worry about it."

"Growing on govermint property, that's some real

time, man. Don't worry about it? Shitfire. You think he's
gettin' back at you for her cheatin' with you?"

"That was ten years ago, Cobb. They weren't even
married. Anyway, I found her clothes out there and
took 'em to Loud Thunder park. That should focus the
search over there."

"If they find 'em."

"They will."

Sure enough, on the news from Kansas City that
night, there was a tip about the missing LaCygne woman's partially burned clothing turning up at Loud Thunder,
and off they went to search that area. Waves of people
kneeing through the cheatgrass, horse trailers in the parking lot, no clues found. Then, like most of those searches,
it sort of dried up when the excitement died down and
nobody stumbled over a corpse. After the media exposed
the seamier side of her life, there were no candle-light
vigils for her. TIPS hotline didn't yield anything and it all
sort of blew over. Raleigh was questioned at length but
with no body and a couple of questionable cohorts alibi-
ing for him, the small sheriff's department cold cased it
pretty quick.

I couldn't tell Mary Ellen about it. She thinks we're
all jack-pine savages down in the refuge anyway, but
she's interested in us with her anthropology degrees. We
come from French fur trappers who settled all along the
Little Blue and the Missouri and the Marais Des Cygne
way over a hundred years ago. She finds that fascinating.

I find her fascinating, so it works out. I threw some French at her once in a while, making sure I pronounced it right. Old lady Chouteau in LaCygne at the Refuge Tavern coached me in French. Her people explored Kansas in the 1700s. Most people around here pronounce it "lay-seen" but not her. Anyway, she explained how to drop the last letter of certain words and how to form the word while saying it. Sometimes you have to hold your mouth funny to say it right. When Mary Ellen spoke French to me, I nodded and smiled, not understanding a word of it. Or I said "*Mais oui, mais oui*" in an absent-minded way and pretended I was looking for something under the bed, something I couldn't find and which caused me to say, "*Zut alors!*" I didn't fool her but she loved me for trying.

So, Mary Ellen was asleep and I was awake but drowsing luxuriously the morning Raleigh showed up. My aunt Vinita was in Oklahoma visiting her sister in, you guessed it, Vinita, the town she was named for. A few minutes later I was thankful she was gone for the weekend. I heard some horn honks out there and the dogs raising hell. We've got two biters, blue heelers. The rest of the dogs are hounds that just make noise and then look around like, "Where am I?"

I got up, slipped on some cargo shorts and my sneakers, and, yawning, went on down the shaky spiral staircase and out the back door which faces the gravel drive.

It was Raleigh's truck. Cobb had the two heelers under control and Raleigh was standing by his open door.

"What can I do for you, Raleigh?" said Cobb.

Not friendly, not unfriendly. Raleigh was not highly regarded anywhere that I knew of. Cobb's neutrality seemed ominous. It was unusual for anyone to venture into the compound uninvited. I tensed up. Was Pete here? I wondered. That question was answered as he came ambling up from the metal shop building, wiping his greasy hands on a pink industrial rag.

"Raleigh," he said, "Shit it ain't noon yet, what are you doin' up so early?"

"Funny," said Raleigh. "I'll get right to the point, boys." Then he just stood there as if he forgot what he was going to say.

Cobb and Pete both cocked their heads, like they were trying to hear some far off music, or like, "Yeah?"

Raleigh's unkempt hair shot out from under a grimy John Deere gimme cap and his beard was between needing a shave and growing out for real. The gun rack in his back window held a cane that he used to prod livestock through the chute at the auction center in town. He was red eyed and both his hands were jammed into a light hooded sweatshirt that he didn't need on such a warm morning.

That's when I suddenly figured he had a gun in one pocket. I suppose Cobb and Pete knew right off. I was behind him, and unnoticed, so I started moving up closer to him. Pete gave me a shake of the head, no, so I stayed where I was. Pete was a ranger in the army and had been in lots of fixes back in the day.

But there was always that final fix, I remember thinking.

"I know you knew where LeAnne is," Raleigh said.

"Wish I could help you there, Raleigh, but she's probably in Denver or somewhere by now," Pete said.

"Think she's alive, do you?"

Pete didn't reply, just stood there looking at Raleigh, still fooling with the shop rag. Cobb's hands hung by his sides, slightly out from his body. I could feel the tension in my neck, my knees.

"I know she's not," Raleigh said, and he smiled—or tried to.

I got the idea he was trying to be cool in his own little movie here.

"What I'm here about is a business thang," he continued.

Pete just laughed, more like blowing some breath out with a smile.

"I want in on the LaCgyne Green," Raleigh said. "Half."

"Why, Raleigh, they ain't no such thing. LaCygne Green is a myth."

"Or else, I'll get some search parties going on a brand new tip that she's buried somewhere back in that marsh you like so much," Raleigh said, gesturing with his head back over by the lake.

"Better do that, then. The other fairy tale ain't workin'."

"Hot damn you, Pete, think you're so fuckin' cool!"

That's when Raleigh pulled the gun, but it hung up on the sweatshirt pocket by the hammer and, in trying to get it loose, he fired it wild somewhere into the ground between him and Pete.

Right on the echo of that report, another shot came from where Pete was. Then another. He'd had a snub nose in the shop rag. He was standing sideways, aiming carefully, one hand at his side, like in a duel. The shot made a popping sound. The first shot had confused Raleigh, being just birdshot in a .38 shell, but it had gotten him in the head and shoulders, little blood spots blossoming on his forehead.

The second one got him in the left chest and down he went. The more intelligent hounds had vacated the area, but one of them was interrupted in mid-scratch and sat there with the hind scratching leg sticking up in the air.

"Move his truck into the barn, Travis," Pete said, walking toward Raleigh's downed form. "Now!" he said, when I just stood there.

Raleigh's truck was filthy and smelled of booze and cigarette smoke. Beer cans rolled around in the bed. I thought of something Cobb had said, way in the past, when someone had brought up Raleigh as a useless, mean prick. "No shortage of Raleighs in this world," he'd said.

When I got back, Raleigh wasn't there anymore. I

didn't know how to process what I'd seen. One less Raleigh in this world. The one hound that had stuck around was sniffing the ground where he'd been. I figured I'd better check on Mary Ellen since she'd not come down to see what the racket was. My knees were beginning to shake. I'd have fucked up the confrontation. He'd have gone back to town, talked to anyone who'd listen about the marijuana and where it was. I'd have gone to jail. Etcetera. I'd just seen Pete kill a man, and not in a panic either; he'd been clear-eyed and calm. Man! I climbed the spiral stairs to the sun-flooded bedroom. Holy shit, oh dear.

"Bring me sweet rolls, sweet boy?" she sat up, stretched, looking beautiful, her small white breasts contrasting with her tan. "Petit pains sucres?"

"*Mon dieu!*" I slapped my forehead. "I forgot. I have something better." She hadn't heard the honking or the shots. "Listen, I've been thinking about going back to school." She perked up, interested. "Even moving to KC. To be close to school and you. What do you think?"

STRONG, THE PINK

S trong was a lot of things. He fought Golden Gloves in high school and tried to get Teale to fight, but Teale didn't like getting the shit kicked out of him by some skinny Black kid at the Salvation Army gym in downtown Kansas City. He also hated sparring with Strong, because, though they were friends, Strong was a serious fighter and didn't pull any punches with him. Teale understood this and didn't want to appear less than manly, but he said no to any more boxing. Back in the '50s they didn't wear protective headgear and the club refs didn't really care what went on with the kids.

Besides the pain, Johnny Teale didn't want his face changed around too much, as girls seemed to like it the way it was. Maybe a little scar on his cheek, or over an eye would be neat, but he could probably get that from the crazy way Strong drove his 1941 Chevy. At least he wouldn't have to experience the dry mouth and the trembling knees that pre-fight jitters gave him. All the kids his weight and age at the gym were bad news. Strong would coach him before the one-minute rounds but, once in the ring, he was pre-psyched and ended up with his gloves in front of his face just trying to keep from being punched in the nose.

Lee Strong was also a Pinkerton his senior year in high school. He called it being a pink. It was kind of like being a private detective. He and Teale would go to one or several of the Katz Drugstore chain after school and time the soda jerks after ordering iced tea or cokes. They could get hamburgers, too, or BLTs. All Strong had to do was keep the receipts and Pinkerton paid them. Strong kept a record of how long the Katz employee took, how they acted, if they loitered or ignored customers, that sort of thing. Teale couldn't believe that such a job was available. Sit around and eat and drink and, if anyone was nasty to you, you had them. In the 1950s this was forward thinking.

Strong also plied his trade in other departments. He even bought Trojan rubbers from a woman employee in the prescription drug area, although they didn't require a prescription. They just kept them out of sight, like Playboy magazines.

"You're nuts!" Teale said.

"What about them?" Strong said, just as loud. Both the transaction and the answer flustered the lady behind the counter, Teale could tell. He knew better than to say that to Strong, as that was his stock rejoinder, and it always embarrassed him, as it did now. Strong grinned as he paid the lady.

Strong's eyebrows were kind of like upside-down Vs, and they gave him a mischievous look, or, at times, a rather amazed demeanor. The tipoff that he was not someone to fool with was his build. He could be pretty scary, looking at some would-be adversary with that amazed look, as though he was thinking, *You really want to fuck with me?* And he did kind of invite attention.

Today, he was wearing some weird kind of pants that reminded Teale of sailor pants. They had a panel in front with buttons on either side and they were tight around the thighs. They even had bell bottoms. Shit, Strong could wear a purple tutu if he wanted but Teale wished Strong wouldn't wear this getup when he was with him. Teale could tell that people were looking at those pants. No back pockets and tight around the butt.

If he'd known Strong was wearing them today, he'd have found some excuse not to be seen with him, but it was too late. Strong had picked Teale up in his Chevy as he was walking home from an impromptu Saturday baseball game in the park near his house. Strong got stuff like those pants in stores around Eighteenth and Vine where the Blacks shopped. Sometimes they went to record stores down there and got used 45 RPM records for a dime that were wild. One of the songs kept running through his mind, "Drinkin' Wine Spodeeodee" by Stick

McGhee and His Buddies. Wild. Stuff you'd never hear on the radio. Maybe Strong was part Black or something. He really seemed to like their talk and clothes and all. Thing is Teale was immediately attracted to the music. It had…danger in it, or something…power maybe. It had drive. They called it rhythm and blues. Some of it was like the new Rock and Roll, but more primal somehow. He wondered if liking the rhythm was a flaw or something. His old man wouldn't tolerate him hanging around that part of town. His old man said they weren't fully real people even. Teale didn't believe that, but he didn't say so, not at home.

Anyway, Strong was one of them, it seemed, when they went down there. They knew him, called him "strongman," and he called them "blood." They even went there at night, to Charlie's Blue Room on session night, Thursdays, when musicians from the audience would get up and play, some of them white people. This was KC in 1957. Things were happening. It was a restless time for Teale.

Strong was cool and at home wherever he went. But he was unpredictable. After they left the Brookside Katz store, and were driving through a residential neighborhood, he gunned the '41 Chev and started knocking over garbage cans that were on the street, left there by the pickup people.

"You're nuts!" Teale shouted, laughing, hanging onto the dashboard.

"What about 'em?" yelled Strong, aiming at another garbage can. After hitting eight or nine of them, sending them crashing and rolling into yards and up onto sidewalks, he suddenly became docile, looking both ways at a stop sign, driving off slowly like an old lady.

Teale loved cars, even that Chevy, and couldn't understand why anyone would dent a fender just jacking around.

It made no sense to him. If he had the car, he'd lower it, put dual Smittys on it, and primer it, for a start. It wasn't a bad car, even though he was a Ford guy. He planned to buy a used Ford V8 flathead when he turned sixteen, a couple of months away.

"You know what a superman is?" Strong was looking straight ahead as he drove.

"Yeah, Clark Kent goes into a phone booth and—"

"No, no," Strong interrupted, only mildly annoyed. "Ever read Nietzsche?"

"We don't have that yet."

"And you won't, either. You have to go to the library. Look up 'existentialism,' too. Look up 'experiential philosophy.' Rimbaud."

"Sure thing, Strong. Next time I'm there."

"Well, you need to *live*. You need *experience* if you're to rise above the proletariat. So we're going to experience a robbery."

"Not me, man. That's wrong."

"Depends. If we rob hoods, it's not wrong. We're

only gonna do it once, for the experience. You have to experience everything, to really be alive."

"Wh—what hoods?"

"Biggs Poolroom, downtown on Twelfth Street. You know it?"

"No."

"It's across from the penny arcade. We're going to go case it, right now."

"But not rob it, right?"

Strong didn't answer. He just shifted into a lower gear and slammed his foot on the accelerator. When he turned a corner, the tires squealed, and Teale was thrown against his door. This was a new one for Teale. Strong often talked about different philosophies and things that were above Teale—the atomic bomb, infinity, time, light speed, and interplanetary travel. But those things were just things to muse on, not put into practice.

This experience thing, where did it come from? It seemed Strong was the most experienced high school senior he knew. Why did he have to rob a pool hall? That made no sense at all.

He'd go along if all they were doing was casing it. That appealed to his sense of adventure and gave him a spine shiver of excitement. It was sort of like when he was a little kid hunting communists, spying on neighbors in his grandmother's old part of town one summer, and watching the McCarthy hearings on the black and white TV. Maybe he'd make a good Pinkerton.

"Just casing this place, right?" he asked Strong.

"Right," Strong said as he shifted down for a red light.

꧁꧂

The pool hall was on a lower level than the street. Strong and Teale descended concrete stairs to the door. An old pawn shop sign with three globes, that hung above the door, had been adapted by painting numbers on the globes, and a sign beneath it said *Biggs' Billiards*. They entered tentatively, their eyes adjusting from the brightness outside, to the semidarkness of the long, largely unadorned room. It was cooler in here though stale with tobacco smoke. Ceiling fans moved slowly. Billiard and pool tables were spaced all the way to the back with green porcelain shaded lamps hanging above them from plain cords that were fed by a conduit that ran along the middle of the high, tin-paneled ceiling.

Two tables near the front were occupied—one by a couple of young toughs in their twenties, with cigarettes dripping from their lips, who eyed the boys with contempt, the other by two businessmen in rolled-up shirtsleeves and loosened ties, whose hats and jackets hung on hooks on the wall.

There were wooden benches in tiers as though for spectators, on one wall. An uneven row of photos hung on the wall above the risers of bleachers.

The man perched at the counter, on a high stool, Biggs himself probably, wore a white shirt with pale raised stripes, buttoned at the neck, and suspenders. He was short, bulky, and his unusually black hair was plastered back with pomade or some out-of-fashion substance that made him look '40s gangsterish, to Teale, who thought Biggs looked dangerous.

"How much?" Strong said.

Biggs folded his arms across his chest and nodded, almost imperceptibly, at a cardboard sign to his right, said out of the corner of his slash mouth, "Snake it'd bit ya."

The hand-lettered sign said, *Straight pool, 25c hr. Billiards reserved, no play, pay up on leaving, no chg less than 1/4 hr. last hr.*

Strong walked past the man. Teale followed, nodding at the man who ignored him. Teale stopped to read inscriptions on some of the photos that hung on the wall, noting that Minnesota Fats had played here. Then he was jostled by one of the toughs who was walking around the table, looking at his shots.

"You looking for trouble, dickhead? Guess what. Here it is." The guy stood his cue against the fat outer rail and shoved Teale into the wall. He then flicked his cigarette at Teale's face but Teale instinctively slapped it away. Before anyone could do anything else, Biggs was between them, surprisingly fast.

"Settle up and get out. We don't put up with tough

guys here." Biggs had the young man in a choke hold and was dragging him toward the door.

At the counter, he told him a sum and was paid by the now-shaken young man who spilled some change and bills on the counter and said, "Jeez, Tony, I didn't mean to. The kid fucked up my shot—"

Biggs resumed his seat. "Out. Don't make me hurt you."

Teale thought he looked like a bullfrog on a toad-stool. The other player quietly set his cue in a rack and followed his companion out the door. The remaining players continued their game, talking in low tones. A closer look at them informed Teale they were not businessmen, as he'd first thought. One wore a flashy watch. The other had on a "Mr. B." collared shirt and a pinky ring that caught the light when he coaxed the cue ball smoothly toward the corner pocket, kissing a striped ball in.

"You went into a good stance to defend yourself," Strong said. "But you don't box in a pool hall. Forget the rules on the street." Teale was shaking, but somehow exhilarated by the narrow escape. "You coulda took him," Strong said, matter-of-factly. "I'll show you a couple ways later. Surefire, if you go quick. That's always the secret. He who hesitates gets his clock cleaned." He picked out a cue and rolled it on the table for true and straight, picked it back up, said, "Rack 'em, streetfight-er."

℘℘℘

While they played, Biggs answered the phone and turned toward the street. Strong ducked down as though to tie his shoe. Teale missed a shot. About thirty seconds later Strong stood, walked around the table looking at his shots.

He said to Teale, in a low voice, "Taped a gun under the table. For when we come back."

Teale's mood dipped, and his face must have shown it.

"Don't worry. When we come back, we'll take it with us. In a week or so. Just checking to see if it's still there. I put it there last week." He grinned, his expressive eyebrows dancing upward.

"You're nuts, Strong."

"What about 'em, Teale?"

The other two men were wearing their fedoras, carrying their coats, leaving. As they settled up with Biggs, Teale heard him say, "Sorry to kick your boys out, Sammy, but rules, you know—"

"No sweat, Tony. They're tryin' a get their bones—impress us. They gotta learn how to behave in public. Good lesson," said the man with the Mr. B. collar, as Biggs helped him on with his suit jacket.

What he couldn't hear was when the other man said, in a lower voice, "I think them two are your table number four gun guys. The one was looking under the table."

One of the men glanced at Teale and Strong.

The one named Sammy, said, "Want us to take care of it?"

"Naw," said Tony. "I unloaded the piece anyway. If they use it, I'll just shoot 'em." They laughed and the other man slipped into his jacket unassisted. They left, and Teale and Strong were the only customers.

Strong handed Teale his keys. "Go get the Chevy. Park at the bus stop around the corner from the penny arcade, heading south. Watch for me. You drive, we'll just drive off slow."

"Aw, no, Lee, don't—"

"You'll just be driving, no big deal. Timing's perfect. I need you, Johnny. You'll see. Slick as a gut."

"Shit, you said—"

"I know. But it's right. It's time. We won't ever do it again--that's when they catch you. Come on, man, you've got the easy part."

Teale felt like he did right before he fought one of the glowering kids at the Salvation Army gym with no referee, just some uncaring guy at the bell. Sometimes they let it go more than a minute, he was sure of it. He flinched a little, when the bright sunlight hit him, stopped on the steps to the sidewalk so his eyes would adjust. In his mind, he tried to rationalize what he, they, were doing, but came up blank. He knew he was crossing some line and would never be able to retract it. It would end up on the minus side. Shortly, he would be a criminal.

They jumped him as he passed the alley on the way to Strong's car. The blow from the sap one of the pool hall toughs hit him with sent him far into a black unconscious state with some red fireballs along the way, but the blade sliding into his liver killed him.

At the pool hall, Strong paid Biggs for the time and replaced his wallet, sailor-like, in his waistband with half of it hanging out.

Something wasn't right about the gun. The tape wasn't the same. Something. Well, at least Teale would get the rush, the experience. He'd tell him later that it was a no-go. He smiled and stood in front of the pool hall for a moment, allowing his dilated pupils to close some before he crossed the busy street to the penny arcade.

EXHUMING CAPTAIN MIDNIGHT

From twelve on, life showed more signs of being the bitch everyone promised it would be. At fifteen, I was old enough to have considered suicide. Wild swings of weirdness—bird-brained hilarity to shadowy melancholy. I couldn't drive legally yet, but I rented motorcycles with my paper route money and a friend's driver's license. I'd seen Marilyn Monroe naked. This was in 1954. The friend, Ray, whose license I borrowed, had shown me the first issue of a magazine called *Playboy* and Ms. Monroe was curled up on a red satin sheet in the altogether. I think it cauterized some part of my brain and turned me into a sex fiend. I never recovered.

So, at fifteen, I was trying to figure out a way to say goodbye to my childhood. A ritual. A viking funeral-like passage. This was a distressing time. I still sort of liked flying model airplanes; hiding behind the big velvet couch waiting, in vain, for someone to sit on the woopee cushion I'd planted there; reading *AIRBOY* comic books while eating a peanut butter and Fritos sandwich. Goodbye Hopalong Cassidy, too. Especially since Ray told me about seeing him at the Shrine Rodeo, in an echoing concrete runway waiting to ride into the arena. He'd smacked his horse in the head and said, "Settle down you lop-eared cocksucker!" Two counts against him. Growing up is painful shit. Acquisition of unwanted knowledge. Ray, of course, thought it was funny.

I decided not to make too big a deal out of the ritual. I would put childish things in a Folger's coffee can, tape it up, wrap it in tinfoil and bury it five steps north and ten steps west of the base of the clothesline post in the back yard of my grandmother's house. It didn't have to be goodbye. It could be a time capsule. Just in case, I would draw a map, so that, years later, I could dig it up. Or maybe the following summer. Or never.

Items:

One Lone Ranger Atomic Bomb glow-in-the-dark ring.

Fifty years later, I questioned such a thing. Really? An atomic bomb on a ring, purporting to be a Lone Ranger artifact? As they say in online shorthand, WTF? But, yes, there was such a thing. Look it up on eBay.

One Little Orphan Annie decoder
the size of a small compact;

One box of roll caps for a cap pistol;
A pack of Black Cat firecrackers;
One tin of Surefire Itching Powder;
A standing liberty quarter, almost smooth;
A mercury dime;
An empty Co2 cartridge;
Six .22 shells;
One Handshake "Joy" Buzzer;
A tiny Popeye flip book;
Three of the best aggie marbles I'd ever owned;
One marble sized "steelie" steel bearing;
An Indian head penny
An aluminum star token stamped with my name,
from Rockaway Beach;
1 shotgun shell, 12 gauge;
One Roy Rogers pocketknife;
One cherry bomb;
A bumper-car pass from Fairyland Park;
A Mexican peso;
A pair of X-ray glasses that were a big gyp;
A Griesedieck Beer bottle cap;
An ad for plans to build a King Midget automobile
from Popular Mechanics;
And last, but no way least, an ornate 1948 Captain Mid-
night Pocket Decoder, with a coded note.

I could only remember the preamble. "I, Thatcher Hornbill, do solemnly...something, something, something." I wanted to read what this fifteen year old Thatcher had to say.

The two decoders in the coffee can unraveled ultimately disappointing commercial messages from Ovaltine, but could be put to other uses involving dirty words and teacher-indecipherable notes in classroom settings. And, of course, my solemn oath of growing up or whatever.

Okay, wipe away some fifty, fifty-five years. Bam. Gone. No shit, just about that fast, too. Women. Children. Homes. Cars. Marriages. Lake houses. Dreams of wild success. Zap 'em. Gone like summer wages. Gone like the wild goose in winter. Hoffa. Casper. Invisible gone.

Stop motion, freeze frame. Screech to a halt. An emotion surfaces. Examine the SOB. Nostalgia, that's what it was. Not the noblest of emotions, yet not unpleasant.

Put that sucker under the lens of a fresh-poured Jack Daniels. Blow it up. Turn up the Spotify of *Moonlight in Vermont*. My god. Those times. Those mellow, slow unbuttoning of blouses, Chanel released from secret places times. Oh. Go back a little farther. Back to boyhood. Backward, turn backward, O Time, in your flight, make me a child again, just for tonight.

It was in that coffee can at my grandmother's old house, my boyhood. When she died, they sold the house. The neighborhood was deteriorating. Car washes, pawn shops, loan sharks opening up storefronts a block away by the old stone Catholic church we'd attend on those warm summer Sunday mornings, Gregorian-like chants and soft bell ringing lulling me to moist open-mouthed sleep, inhaling incense like opium.

If I could find that coffee can, I'd start over, do it all right this time, from fifteen on. I actually believed this.

Have another drink, Thatcher.

Don't mind if I do.

The neighborhood was all Black now. I was all White. Had to figure this out. Mac-tens being the weapon of choice around the old 'hood. I couldn't just march in there, unarmed, with a shovel and start digging. It would require stealth. Nerve.

ᘒᘓᘒ

The next day, a bit hung over, I turned at the corner where the Dairy-Freez used to be. A thrift store occupied the land now. Barred windows. A giant banana sat out front, to draw attention, I guessed. It got mine. It was about two blocks. *To Grandma's house I go.* I drove right by it because it was not the same. There was an asphalt circle drive in the front yard. A For Sale sign in front of that. A rusty white pickup with toolbox sides, ladder racks, sat in the drive. Once turned around, I pulled in, gazed at the stucco house. Looked pretty good, actually. The screened in porch had now become enclosed and part of the house, making it appear bigger, I supposed, though the whole house seemed smaller than it did when I was a boy. I knew that happened, but I was always surprised, wanted to remark on it to someone. My second-story sleeping porch room still had windows all the way around. Dormers, roof, all the same shape. Used to be zinnias, peonies, lilacs all across the front, circling around to the side yard. All gone. The tree that I used to climb down from the sleeping porch room was still there but bigger. Fifty years bigger. Hammering and circle-saw noises from inside brought me back to my mission— reconnaissance. This would be easier than I thought. I could walk right in. And I did.

A couple of workmen, one White, one Black, kept on working. I waited until one paused, looked at me.

"Hi. I used to live here a long time ago. Okay if I go upstairs, look around?"

"Sure, Knock yourself out," the White guy said, resumed cutting a piece of plywood on sawhorses, the circle-saw whining industriously, fresh sawdust smell. The Black guy started a nail in a door frame, banged it home with two satisfying thwacks, hammer held almost loosely in his hand. Why did people say knock yourself out. It was smartass. Gratuitous. Knock *your*self out, dick brain.

The stairs seemed more narrow, although I knew they weren't. I paused at the room where my grandmother died in bed, attended by my aunt and father. She didn't know me. After the funeral, I stopped by the old house and her presence was quite strong for a moment or two.

I passed my old man's room, tiny. Did I smell pipe tobacco? Did his ghost roam these narrow hallways? Did hers? She would play Chopin at the old baby grand, a cigarette in her mouth, long ash drooping, frowning against the smoke curling into her eyes. Swaying back and forth on the bench, hands diving into the keys. What a ghost that would be.

I'd have gone up to the third floor but it didn't interest me. I headed for my old room. It had shrunk along with the rest of the place. Right now, it was just a little side room they called a sleeping porch and now it was full of floor tile, boxes of stuff, fixtures, coils of wire. I tried to imagine the radio going, the fan, the magic of anticipation of a free flight airplane I'd made, affixing the small glo-fuel engine to the firewall, the snort of its first breath of life, the angry whine as it sucked fuel.

I looked out the window to the side yard, my purview in the yearly summer visit to my grandmother's house. The clothesline was long gone, no more posts. There used to be a birdhouse on another post, a marker from which to count steps to the buried coffee can. It was gone, too. As a small child, I shook that post to see the birds that lived in the little house atop it. They were wrens. My wish was granted. Out they came on red alert, pecking at my head, chasing me into the house, me shrieking in the treble ranges. Live and learn. That was my don't-fuck-with-the-birds lesson, even little ones.

I shot a mental azimuth to where the can might be,

fixed the points in my mind. That was when I knew I was serious about this, I was sober, pretty much, even though the Starbucks double espresso I carried had brought a little of the buzz back. I was actually, physically here in this house. Did I believe the can would take me back to age fifteen? My answer surprised me. Sure. Heck, yeah. Stranger things had happened, but not much. There was magic in believing.

I left. The two workmen were somewhere else in the house. Their radio played old Stones. "Mannish Boy." I wondered if the workmen go back and forth between hip-hop and rock and roll. How did they agree on it? Flip a coin? The rapper Fifty Cent came to mind.

In the side yard toward the back, I stood in the approximate area of what I envisioned from the sleeping porch. The back yard had completely changed. Used to be a natural-stone retaining wall to a higher yard and a little jungle-type area separating the yards. I used to climb the wall, cut through Gustafson's yard on my way up to Troost Avenue and the used comic book place. I'd trade comics there, two for one in the musty store. Troost wasn't exactly elegant, even back then.

Okay, the birdhouse post would have been about here. I paced off the steps, taking care to compensate for my adult paces, taking smaller strides. This general area. I looked about for something to stick in the untended lawn. I laid an X of sticks there and snooped around the detritus of rehab laying closer to the house. Aha. A rusty wire with a tattered Day-Glo pennant that must have been used to mark water lines or something. I jabbed it into the earth where the X was. I'd bring a metal detector if I could find one. Or not.

Witnesses might think there was buried treasure, wait until I unearth it, kill me. The whole deal was problematic. If I only had a shovel, I could dig right here and now, get the hell out. But I'd have to come back. I felt like a ghost drifting around here.

დოდ

One night. Two. Jack Daniels. The old songs. Public TV fundraising with Doo-Wop put me over the top. Now *those* were the days, Thatcher. Heck with it, I was goin' in. Flashlight. Spade. Plastic grocery bag in case the can had disintegrated. Work gloves. Pistol? No, I'd talk my way out. Cops, neighbors, I'd think of something on the way over. A plausible story. I looked at my watch. 10:15 p.m. The time of night put limits on plausibility.

I'd take my wife's quiet Civic but, since she passed away, I never renewed the plates. Okay, the Volvo wagon with the gutter muffler. Should have fixed that. *Just go.*

Troost at night. Women in shorts and halter tops walking. Leaning into car windows, music booming out of the cars. How could they even hear each other?

Not my problem. I turned at the banana, drove slowly to the old house, parked on the street. No signs of life

at the house—dark, driveway empty. I located the wire
with the pennant in the shadows.

The streetlight beam was blocked by the corner of
the house. Good, I'd be digging in the dark. I chunked the
spade into the ground, tossed aside a little pile of dried
dirt and grass. Again. I was warming to this.

"Don't fucking move." Then a strong light. A dog's
growl on top of this.

"Oh shit," I said, quickly, involuntarily.

"Thass the dog's name," the voice said. "So many
people have called him that, he answers to it." Maybe a
chuckle. "Drop the shovel."

I did. But I didn't put my hands up. This might be it.
Program, as an army buddy used to say. I turned slowly
toward the light. The voice sounded like Samuel L. Jackson in *Pulp Fiction*. The light dipped to the dog on a
choke chain and leash. Pit bull, all teeth and sinus noises.
Then the light flashed on a nickel-plated Desert Eagle.
Light back in my eyes. I supposed he was holding the
fucking .45 sideways.

My eyes, accustomed now to this apparition, relayed
to me that his flashlight was on a headband, dog leash in
left hand, big stupid gun in right hand.

"Dog also answers to 'Fuck me, I'm outa here,' and
'I think I shit my pants.' He likes the first one as it means
a chase, and he *always* wins." Chuckle for sure.

Suddenly, I was tired of this. "Fuck you, your dog,
and your Desert Eagle. What a stupid fucking weapon to

carry around. You rob fast food places? Hold it sideways and scream like a little girl to open the cashbox?"

Silence. Dog sits down.

"I am not the perpetrator here," the guy said quietly.

"And me with my sp—shovel, I am? You got gold back here? Bodies?"

"It's my yard, dawg. It's night time. People get killed around here just for showin' up. White man with a shovel. Man." The light on his forehead swung back and forth sadly as he shook his head. "Mm-mmmp."

"Look, let me dig about a foot deep, find what I'm after, and I'll just scamper on home. After replacing the divot, of course."

He sighed heavily. "White people." The light swept back and forth again. "All right. Dig." His "all right" came out "aaiight." He walked to the front porch, came back without dog or gun. He now had a long cop-looking flashlight which he trained on the beginning of the hole. No weapon was apparent but I was not going to test that assumption.

I put out my hand. "Thatcher Hornbill."

"Really?" It comes out as a laugh. "Sorry. Mine's Rayondo Renard."

"Rayondo? Sugar Ray Renard, the fighter?"

"Used to be," he said.

I forgot my dry mouth, the slight tremor in my knees. "Damn. I followed you in the Olympics. And after, of course. Wow. You were fantastic!"

"The past. I don't dwell on it."

"That last fight with Trumbull. You out-boxed him, out-classed him, held him up at the end—"

"Like I say, all in the past. What are you digging up here?"

I felt rebuked, and something else. Maybe silly. The welterweight champ was dismissing his own past, and I was looking for trinkets in a Folger's can.

"A sort of time capsule." I told him about the contents of the can, the decoders, the circumstances surrounding the burial.

"Captain Midnight," he said. "That's you."

I continued digging. It was obvious the hole was going to produce nothing.

"Look," he said. "Why not come back in the daytime. I know where I can borrow a metal detector. Tomorrow after ten a.m., ten thirty, okay?"

I left the shovel. We shook hands again. He watched while I walked to the station wagon, started it, drove away. Maybe he was taking my license number but I didn't think so. Sugar Ray Renard. A hero of mine. I drove home, west and south to the suburbs. He was obviously part of the vanguard moving into the somewhat blighted areas, renewing, resettling. He was about ten years younger than I was. I watched his career arc up, then suddenly plummet like so many fighters. But he'd kind of disappeared. No articles or TV mentions of him that I'd seen. Sugar Ray Robinson came out on a US stamp, another hero of mine. But Sugar Ray Renard vanished. Now we were digging in his yard. A horn sounded behind me at a stoplight that had turned green. I waved, lurched ahead.

As I pulled into my driveway, I turned off the ignition and thought. Sugar Ray was a young sixty or maybe fifty-five, somewhere in there. Still working probably, at whatever ex-fighters did when they vanished from the ring. Opened a gym? Worked at UPS? Who knew? That house wasn't cheap. And if he was the one rehabbing it, he had to have some bucks. I hoped so, for some reason. Inside, I poured bourbon into a faceted glass. My hand shook as I lifted it to my mouth.

 හත

I pulled into the smallish circle driveway a few minutes before the appointed time. A Cadillac Escalade with black-tinted windows sat in the semi-circle of asphalt. Hanging from the rearview mirror were a pair of miniature boxing gloves. Sugar Ray appeared to be doing well.

He came out, dog and a shambling sort of person with him, a kid? Looked like a kid.

Sugar Ray motioned to me to get out of my car, walked closer. "This may be distasteful to you, but it calms everything down, both the dog and the kid see it and think everything's okay—we have to hug is all and laugh a little bit, then they cool their jets, and life goes on at the Renard household."

"Ahh. Not at all distasteful. I'd be hugging one of my heroes. Had you been older, and me younger, I'd have had your poster on my side of the bedroom door. As it was, I had Annette Funicello. And, later, what's her face with the feathery hair and big tits."

He laughed, I laughed, we hugged, patted one another's backs, eyes on the kid and dog. The dog immediately lost interest, wandered off, and peed on my tire, the boy stood and clapped his hands sort of, something off about the boy, young looking, maybe ten, maybe twelve, but large, maybe even obese, but his face was that of a Down Syndrome person.

I was taken aback, hadn't ever thought of it, since I'd never seen a Down Syndrome Black kid, would have, if questioned, opined that there wasn't such a thing, that only Whites, maybe Asians, were susceptible—wasn't the term at one time, way back in my childhood, mongoloid?—and there hadn't been many, period. It hadn't seemed to have happened back then, just as cancer had not seemed like a prevalent disease. At any rate, here he was, a Black Down Syndrome kid, I was sure of it. He had that slightly distracted look, a sweetness about him that invited the kind of hug his father and I had just shared. His father? I didn't know that. I would wait for any explanation if one was forthcoming, otherwise I'd just shut up.

Sugar Ray turned to the boy. "C'mere, hon, want you to meet someone."

The boy advanced, shyly, looking down, sideways, anywhere but at me. Then he fixed me with that look, through glasses. "Hello."

"Hello," I said, too quietly, cleared my throat, said it too loudly.

"This here is Cap'n Midnite," Sugar Ray said. "Shake."

The boy put out his hand. "Foyd. Mah name." We shook.

"Floyd," said his father, to me. "After guess who."

"Aahh, Patterson," I said. "Great name indeed."

"He's a sweetheart, Floyd is. My man." He put his arm across Floyd's ample shoulders. "Seventeen. Docs said he wouldn't make it past twelve. It's him and me."

"I did." Floyd beamed. "Fav yeos." He held up a hand. "How old Cah Midnite?"

"Up there, Floyd. Do this ten, twenty times." I opened and closed my palms again and again. "Too many."

"Too many?" He seemed incredulous. "Nah too many, no," he said seriously.

"Life is pretty important to Floyd," Sugar Ray said. "He wants me to live to be a hundred. Right?"

"Den you kin dah," said Floyd.

"Thank you, hon."

It was obvious they had discussed this at length. I felt

close to tears. Old people have to watch that shit, we cry easily. I cried at *Peanut Vendor* by Stan Kenton when it played on a late night jazz station. It was a song Fran and I had heard for the first time at a Kenton concert way back in the '50s, at Swope Park. Funny, I could remember everything about that balmy humid night—the breeze, the flash of the brassy music, the drive home in my old Ford. Yet I could hardly remember what fucking day it was and when I had a dental appointment.

"Well, hon, go get that metal detector, and be careful bringing it, go slow okay? It's not ours so we have to be extra careful."

"Okay" Floyd clapped his hands softly and spoke some words as he walked to the house, taking this mission seriously, as he probably should. I knew nothing of metal detectors other than that they seemed expensive, possibly fragile. The dog was ambling along with him, wagging his tail and looking up at him, sensing this could possibly have a fun component. And maybe it could.

"Floyd's Special Olympics, a swimmer."

"Do Special Olympics kids box?" I asked before I thought better of it.

"Special Olympians don't need to," he said. "They're tough all on their own. A non-threatening tough, you know? Better than us."

I nodded, compressed my lips, hoping to look thoughtful.

Boy and dog and metal detector emerged from the

house, dog sniffing whatever parts of the instrument he could reach, interested. A pit bull never looked less frightening than this one, almost comical in its puppy-like enthusiasm. Something was up and he wanted in.

Floyd handed Sugar Ray the appliance with both hands, as though proffering a ceremonial sword to a candidate. Sugar Ray took it.

"Thank you, hon. Let's get this show on the road."

"Show on th roh." Floyd adjusted his glasses with the classic one-fingered push at the bridge.

Sugar Ray turned the appliance on, donned the headset, made some minor adjustments, then began sweeping the area with the detector plate about an inch off the ground. He looked at us and smiled as he walked, seemingly aimlessly about. He tossed a penny on the ground, swept over it, grimaced as it shrieked shrilly enough that I could hear it from the headset. "Son of a bitch works," he said.

"Suvva bidge works," Floyd said to the dog, who was clearly pleased. Floyd moved from foot to foot in anticipation.

"Here, you try for a while, Thatcher." Sugar Ray removed the headset, handed the whole rig to me. "You know where you buried the thing. Generally."

"Very generally. I might start over by where the wall was, and sweep systematically."

I put the headset on, adjusted it, swept over the penny for a baseline sound. Sqwaaawk. The dog cocked his head. Nothing, no sounds, then a peep or two. Turned out to be a pop-top tab just under the soil.

I worked outward from the wall, wider and wider, then I heard it, strong and steady in one spot.

"Shovel," I shouted. "Please," I amended.

Sugar Ray handed the shovel to Floyd who turned it over to me, gravely.

I took a deep breath. Floyd mimics the breath. Sugar Ray held both hands up with fingers crossed. The dog whined.

The soil here was sandy and a couple of shovelfuls removed the dirt from a small object, not a coffee can. It's a bottle opener. Rusty and old, but by scraping my thumbnail across the etched lettering I could read Smitty's Tap, and an address in Independence, Missouri. I handed it to Sugar Ray.

Finally, Floyd was sweeping the device around haphazardly when he apparently heard a signal, and homed in on it. He dropped the metal detector and began digging with his hands. The dog joined in, throwing dirt backward between his legs, stopping, sniffing, starting again, whining. I took the shovel and joined them. It was the time capsule. I pulled it gingerly out of the hole. It wasn't buried very deep. The tinfoil was filthy and fell apart easily, but the can had retained some of its color, though rusted. The tape covered areas were intact, and the tape pulled apart fibrously.

"Wait. Go no farther," Sugar Ray said. "This is a fifty-year-old time capsule. First we get a table cloth or something to empty it onto. And a cold beer. Bud, Thatcher?"

"You bet. Bud. And Floyd?"

"He gets a Diet Rite, he likes those. Makes him belch. And that makes him laugh. Don't open anything while I'm gone. Thatcher?"

"I won't." I put my hands in the air. Floyd did the same.

⃝꙰⃝

Floyd did belch and laugh. We all laughed. Then Sugar Ray flourished a sheet on the ground. I dumped the contents of the Folger's can on the sheet, but carefully. Magical pieces of the past clinked and rustled, artifacts of Mu or Atlantis couldn't be any more fascinating. Sugar Ray reached for one of the coins, then hesitated, looked a question at me.

"Sure, go ahead."

"Man, this is old. Standing liberty," he said.

"It was old when I had it. I gave coins like that to the ice cream truck guy."

"Bud Lightyow! Bud Lightyow!" Floyd exclaimed. He was looking at the Captain Midnight decoder. I looked at Sugar Ray.

"Buzz Lightyear, he's saying. His favorite character from *Toy Story*. Looks a little like that."

I could see Floyd was excited, but he was keeping his hands off for now, almost dancing in his desire for this piece. It was also the piece I most wanted to examine, to rub as though a genie's lamp. I wanted to read the coded piece of paper that had survived with it, see what gibberish I had written as a kid. I handed it to Floyd and he looked at me. "Bud Lightyow for me?"

"For you," I said.

Sugar Ray was perturbed. "Naw, Thatcher, it's part of your childhood stash, man, you can't—"

"Look at him," I said. "Do *you* want to take it away?"

Sugar Ray smiled, shook his head.

Floyd patted the decoder, held it next to his cheek. He examined it closely, sat down in the grass with it. He was in another world.

"I can't remember making anyone that happy in years. It's his."

❦❦❦

Someone called to me. It was my grandmother. It was time for church. Last week I hid in the bushes by the little wall and they gave up, went without me. My aunt, my grandmother, my dad, they all climbed into the old '41 Dodge and left. And there were no consequences. They just figured I was playing somewhere out of earshot. I grabbed the taped-up Folger's can, the shovel, and con-

cealed myself in the bushes. They called again, halfheart-
edly. Then I heard the car's gears grind as they pulled out
to the street.

I came out, peered around the corner of the screened-
in porch. They were gone. I felt a little guilty, but not too
much. I'd gotten my white Sunday shirt dirty somehow.
My blue pants had dirt at the knees. I placed the can into
the hole and shoveled dirt over it, replacing the grass and
patting it firmly in place.

 espen

It was a mystery to Sugar Ray where Floyd got the
odd—obviously old—object with the space suit guy on it.
He called it his Buzz Lightyear but it was really nothing
like the *Toy Story* plastic toys they got for his birthday. It
was metal and tarnished and old. It said Captain Midnight
Decoder. Sugar Ray felt a strong current of deja vu, then
it passed.

"Where did you get this, Floyd?"

"You frien. Cah Midnaht."

"Oh, let him keep it," said Maddy, the boy's special
needs companion, laying the day's mail on the kitchen
table. She forgot to tell Rayondo she'd had to sign for one
letter from a law office.

Sugar Ray handed the object back to Floyd, and as
he did so a tightly folded piece of paper that was taped to
it came loose. He unfolded it carefully, saw a series of

numbers. That night after Floyd was in bed, he took the decoder object from the bedside table, sat in the kitchen with a pencil and paper, and turned the wheel of the decoder to the letters that corresponded to the numbers.

"I, Thatcher Hornbill, do solemnly put to rest my childish shit, not knowing what lays ahead, maybe riches, maybe death, maybe Marilyn Monroe touching my ferndike."

Sugar Ray was laughing, trying not to laugh too loud, wheezing, the laughter coming out in gasps. What a white name, Thatcher fucking Hornbill. Marilyn Monroe, oboy. This was something. Ferndike. He shook his head, his shoulders bobbing with laughter he was trying to hold in. The dog laid his head on Sugar Ray's thigh, looking up at him, sensing merriment.

Upstairs in his bedroom, he laid his change on the dresser, not noticing the worn standing liberty quarter among the coins. The dog padded into Floyd's room, lay down by the side of the bed. Sugar Ray brushed his teeth as the TV in his dark bedroom flickered and a night newscast mentioned, in passing, the death of TL Hornbill, prominent insurance executive who had died in his sleep the previous week. A controversy was stirring among some distant relatives about a new will he'd had drawn up.

DESERT DOG

I'm a rover and a rambler and a high desert gambler!"
I sing snatches of things I make up and real songs
quite loud, quite loud in my Kenworth tractor Desert
Dog with its GPS and satellite wireless, Bluetooth, computer screen, DVD-player and iPod station, and a high
octane CD sound system that equals any luxury boat on
the road. I am Hooked Up. I can listen or I can sing, or
both. I love it.

"You have the most *awful* singing voice," Priscilla
says, with real astonishment but with smiling affection.
"A cross between an even more tuneless Johnny Cash
and bad George Jones karaoke."

It sounds fine in my head. She puts up with it in good
humor. She is a school teacher and has such patience. A
wonderful trait along with hotness which she also possesses. Lucky kids in her class spend more time with her
than I do.

I am sitting at the top of an icy-looking hill, idling, in the foothills of the Rockies heading east, the kind of hill that's a brake-killer on good days and this is not your good day. I want to get to the flatlands and make some time.

It's dusk, cloudy drizzle, thirty degrees, weather lowering. I look down this long winding snake-ass thing and I see my death, and the fear rises in my thorax. I don't know exactly what a thorax is but it seems like a cross between my throat and my esophagus or something that would carry bile up the tube and spread it around like evil under my tongue and I'd swallow it back down, leaving an aftertaste of burnt truck stop coffee and bacon. Maybe ozone. I think, *Why* did I take this up, this over-the-road madness? I am a huge flaming fireball of a news story waiting to happen, then the pretty girl with rosy cheeks and pumped-up lips looks at the male anchor she's messing with and says, and now for a lighter look at…what, maybe a secret Santa story.

I can't back up. And if it's icy, there's no way I can steer through this serpentine slither without at the very least jack-knifing and shearing trees, guardrails punching through the saddle tanks, and—

"Shoot," I say, pulling out onto the roadway, "here we go, you sonsabitches," addressing my humorless dad and my grandpa, "I'll see you in hell in about one minute and a half." Gears up, speed gaining, nothing coming, I take the whole middle of the road.

I ease off as I head down, hoping Desert Dog don't break traction, no turning back now, I'm all in. I tap the brakes, just tap them, air from the system shushing me in an angry little psshht. No yawing or slewing, no thorax-sickening, sphincter-tightening spinal frisson. *Like* that frisson, Priscilla. What a *word*! Like your *Freixenet* champagne. Chills. Up your spine, down your gullet, my girl Priscilla uses words like a poet. She teaches English, gaining speed, can't gear down, hit a skate of black ice. Oohhhhh shitfire. No, she's straight, she's moving, the road ain't iced, just that one black-ice bad-ass patch, hanging onto the curve, not so snaky as it looked from up on top.

Whoa, shit dawg, now we're talkin'. Desert Dog is gonna make 'er. I got her name feather-ghost striped on the doors. Shines in the sun in a leaded glass blue and blue-green against the dark blue. Oh, man, we did it, faced the abyss and beat the bitch.

I snap open a CD, one-handed, Joe Bonamassa, slide it into the player slit which sucks it in like…well, I can't say, as Priscilla does not like the metaphor, but it makes me smile and affects me well below the thorax, I'll say that. I turn it up and Joe wails, *wails*, plays that thing like a banshee in heat in Dante's hell circle number three. "Oh my," I say out loud. "Oh *my*."

Black smoke a-blowin' over eighteen wheels, I am feeling it in my blood which flows like good synthetic forty-weight oil at 190 degrees, viscosity, just right. I am steady as she goes rollin', workin' for the man ever night and *day*.

I hear myself laughing. Sometimes I talk. I say my dailies when driving, prayers for Priscilla, for the dogs, our home, our safety. I always sing. Joe makes me want to dance but I can't bounce around too much in DD. She likes a precision driver. And then there's the load all chain-boomered down on the bed, hauling power plant sections tarped and ominous, looming and official like a government load of something they don't want you to know. But it just looks thataway, those black tarps flappin'.

Load of doom. Doomload download at Alton or East St. Louis. Let me outa these Colorado Rockies. Across the plains. Flamelicks from the blues virtuouso Bonamassa the master bender of Fender. But I don't know what he plays, Gretsch, Gibson, what. Matters not. He could make a Chinese banjo quote Shakespeare.

☙❧

Kansas. Flat and windswept with Priscilla's Capote lurking, licking his lips still looking at Klutter luck or lack and…Hank Jr. sings, as do I, "Hey, little water boy bring the buck, buck, bucket down, *quack, quack*." Always makes me laugh, lifts my spirits, good thing on this flatland wheat-land weed-land express.

Truck stop looms, Desert Dog and I dust it, shine it,

don't intertwine it, flashing by. I back off and the pipes rap at the waitress there who—maybe tired, maybe worried about a mammogram, maybe her kid sassed her—told me to eat shit and die when I questioned the freshness of the pie. Everyone has bad days, I said to her, and she said sorry, and I tipped her fat, but it leaves me sad, so I pass. Another one in fifty miles, forty minutes. I check my radar detector. It's flashing red, red, red, means only that it's on.

I dial from Jim Rome to Dave Ramsey to Rush Limbaugh. They seem flat as the Kansas-scape, I think Elvis! Yes, "Blue Christmas without you." My phone rings. I snatch it up, pull the charger connection out of it. It's Priscilla.

"Hey," I say.

"Where are you?"

"Truckin' through Kansas but don't tell my momma, she thinks I'm a piano player in a whorehouse."

"Funny."

"Uproarious. Knee-slapping. Side-spl—"

She interrupts. "Be serious for just a second."

"Like a doggone heart attack."

I hear her blow nose air sort of like a laugh but not quite. "When are you home?"

Home being California, the high desert, actual location Hemet. Home in Hemet.

"I will be in Hemet, California 9:16 p.m. December twenty-second."

"Perfect."

'Better than perfect. Unless, of course, you forget my present and are dressed up to go out instead of butt nek-kid."

"We *are* going out during the holidays, truck boy. And you *will* look nice."

"We are and I will. Tell me something sexy."

"Old truckers never die, they just get a new Peter-bilt."

"That's old."

"So are you." She laughs.

Can she be disparaging of my age, the difference in years between us?

"I've been reading the books you gave me," I say.

"Good. Which one are you reading now?"

"That one by Kant about reason."

"Really? I don't remember giving you any philoso-phy books."

"I made that up. Me and Wikipedia."

"You goofball. I've got to go. I love you."

"I love you too."

"Blue Christmas" swells in the cab, all the better be-cause mine won't be blue. Mine will be sun streaming in the venetian blinds, lolling in bed, and then cooking brunch and the dogs bumping around me. Opening pack-ages. I have gotten her presents at Neiman Marcus in Dallas, DD idling at the loading dock in back.

"Blooooo bloooo Christmas without yoooo." Elvis

smirks and dimples as he croons and moons and DD is humming at an eighty sweet spot and Kansas will soon be a memory into Missouri, east to Alton Illinois.

I light up a 420 Marley. I holler around it, "I'm a smoker, I'm a toker, I'm a midnight broker, I'm a joker, and a Fokker and an Absaroker." This rig cost me, but if you live in one half the time, be happy. Desert Dog makes me happy. Lights everywhere, blue dots in back, illegal maybe but nobody says anything. Sleep compartment, I keep it clean, like to sleep in comfort, shower at stops—when the money's good, in good motels, prime rib and a Manhattan on the rocks, read myself to sleep.

"Lap of luxury," Priscilla says about some things.

Her lap *is* luxury and I'm a luxury-hound. She doesn't like too much referencing of the hot spot, the blue dot, the fox trot. But she inspires me, leads me, educates me.

It's not like she is trying to improve me—she just likes teaching. And I'm raw stock she can make something out of. She says I'm smart. Nobody ever told me that. It's great to have a teacher who cares. They say you remember the good ones all your life. This is especially true of me, a teacher's pet for sure.

Whoa, shit, some little sporty number passing me and my radar detector is squawking Smokey X-band, there goes *that* guy's Christmas bonus. Yes, here he comes hot on his ass. Nailed in Kansas in the unsympathetic wheat stubble!

Me and the Desert Dog hauling ass and power plant parts. I hit the all-windows-down button, fresh clean razor-cold Kansas air jets the cab, scrubs the cigar smoke from the plastics, leathers, and chromes, freezes my earring.

A little kid in the back of a Volvo wagon pumps his arm, I give him two blasts of DD's double airs. He claps his hands. We both laugh. It's Christmas.

WHAT WADE CLOVER DID
THE SUMMER OF 1958

Wade Clover was made to work down in the stagnant, humid air of the sweltering coffer-dam as a sort of punishment. But what the foreman, LaWayne DeFeo, didn't know was that Wade preferred it. He loved it, actually. While down there in the airless pit, its steel-encased sides oozing foul-smelling primordial Oklahoma mud at the seams, he'd discovered a way to handle a two-man job all by himself. And this had caught the eye of the field super, Ken Burdock, who told LaWayne that Wade would soon be his equal, in line for a foreman position. Which caused LaWayne to grind his teeth, make fists.

"You okay, LaWayne?" Ken said.

"Fine. Just dandy. Thanks for askin'."

"Thought you were having a seizure of some kind."

"Naw." LaWayne watched the superintendent stride off, kicking up red dust as he headed for the air-conditioned business office, a trailer set into a clearing in the tangled jungle-like wilderness.

LaWayne hated Wade, fucking college student working in the summer, then just as the shit weather turned and got more pleasant, off he'd go to some cushy campus, all monied up from the summer, spend it on pussy and beer and brag about how he'd built a bridge across Lake Texoma. And it was *art* school, to boot. What the hell kind of grownup job does that prepare anyone for?

LaWayne had banished Wade to the cofferdams with the biggest air hammer he could find, told him to cut off the steel-reinforced concrete pilings at the engineers' marks about two foot from ground level.

Cutting piles was, essentially, a two man job, one man bulling the heavy body of the hammer, holding it sideways, chisel end horizontal to the piling, the other man operating the chisel and cutting around the column. The exposed ends of the piles were anywhere from eight to fifteen feet tall, and four feet in diameter. That fucking Wade had looked at the job, clambered back up the rickety ladder, got himself a rope from the supply trailer, and climbed back down.

LaWayne watched, eyes slits, lower lip pushing hard against the upper. Wade tossed the rope over the top of the piling, secured it. He tied the other end to the air chisel so it swung freely about two feet off the ground. Then he pulled his goggles over his eyes, aimed the pneumatic tool end at the piling, and began to cut, concrete chips flying. When he'd hit reinforcing steel, he'd move over, cut some more. LaWayne kicked what he thought was a dirt clod but it was the stub of an old tree root sticking out of the ground and it damn near broke his foot. He hopped around like a wounded crow, cursing.

By the end of the day, the pilings looked like a concrete-chewing team of beavers had been at them, ready for the welders to come and cut the re-bars and knock them over. The worst thing was, the super had gone down into the hole to ask Wade what he was doing, came back up with a smile on his face, so LaWayne couldn't take credit for the idea. The damn kid was always coming up with stuff like that.

The next day, one cofferdam closer to the lake, Wade chipped away in his green-goggled world, singing at the top of his voice. Al Hibbler's "Unchained Melody," with all the high parts. Nobody could hear him anyway with the machine gun rattle of the air chisel.

LaWayne appeared now and then at the edge of the cofferdam, hollering down at him to climb up, perform some make-work task. Wade ignored him, erasing his words with the violence of the hammer, concentrating on the fissures appearing in the concrete. LaWayne would soon go away, figuring it was too much trouble and beneath his station to climb down and wallow around in the mud to get Wade's attention. He'd throw a dirt clod, but the field super would yell at him about safety and the new outfit OSHA that was becoming such a pain in the ass. He could shut down the compressor but that would get him chewed out.

About mid-morning, Wade felt eyes on him. He was being watched by someone, but not the foreman. The sun was getting higher, coming on ten o'clock or so, and when he looked up, there were figures silhouetted against the light—three men in suits, jackets over their shoulders, and to one side, away from them and closer to him, a woman. A breathtaking, tanned young woman with a scowl he could see, even though the large sunglasses she wore obscured a good deal of her expression.

She wore a white sheath dress, sleeveless, and the sun behind her revealed a form that rendered her companions invisible. Legs spread some, pulling the skirt taut, her fists on her hips, her feet in spectator pumps, solidly planted. The stance was one males are familiar with by the time they're teens. It said, "I'm pissed and this is going to last." She appeared to be looking straight at Wade.

The suited men paid no attention to her, talking and gesturing off toward the lake where the bridge was headed. Clover was suddenly conscious of his slack-jawed immobility and the emphatic silence from the dormant air hammer. Sounds were filtering down to him. Birds. A generator. The talk of the men. Something like deja vu was disorienting him, dizzying him. This was backwoods wilderness Oklahoma and you didn't see women in white dresses and heels here, thirty miles from the nearest Coke machine.

Somehow he felt as though he'd been in this scene before. He activated the hammer and it almost got away from him, bouncing crazily on the piling. He felt his face flush red beneath the tan and the grime, even then knowing no one could see that with goggles, hard hat, and red clay dirt overlaying his features.

He chiseled for about ten minutes, really getting down on it before he dared look up again. When he did, they were gone, all of them. He shut the hammer off and listened for voices.

The mud beneath him jiggled from the pile driver sinking another piling down the line, the chunky sound coming after the shockwave. Compressors chugged on or off, expelling air. The tracks of a crane being moved clanked and squealed.

He let the air hammer swing free on the rope and climbed up the crude ladder the carpenters slapped together for these holes. Time for a water break, and he wanted another look at the lady in white.

Maybe he'd dreamed it. He fantasized a lot down there in the green-goggled world. Sang to the girls he had known, would know. Time streamed in a different way in the cofferdam and sometimes he wouldn't hear the whistle blow at five o'clock. Once, he continued on until the shut-down compressor ran out of air and he was alone on the job site. Whistle-bit as they say.

It was already above ninety degrees that morning. The ice block had melted in the galvanized Igloo water cooler. He filled his hard hat a quarter full with water and put it on. Next best thing to a shower. Then he swallowed two salt tablets from the dispenser, washed them down with paper cups of the almost cool water.

"Clover, you bonehead, no wonder we gotta fill them fuckin' coolers four times a day. When are you done with the pilings?"

LaWayne's voice seemed unnaturally loud to Wade. Everything did when he stopped hammering. Birdcalls stood out.

"I should be done by approximately 4:59 p.m.," he replied, flashing him a generous smile. He affected a hip-shot stance and flapping hand gesture. LaWayne had tried to get a rumor going that Wade liked boys, and Wade used it to full advantage to end conversations with him quickly.

LaWayne's eyes slid sideways and he exhaled sharply, making a hasty departure. He tried to emulate the super's purposeful walk but his foot still hurt and he appeared to be making way on the deck of a ship in a storm.

Weird way to walk, Wade reflected. *Could it be a visual reference to the tractionless rumor of my fruitiness?*

Wade looked around for the woman in white. Nothing. A lone dust devil on the dirt road into the job site. Sky the color of steam. A sharp whiff of diesel fuel.

He crumpled the paper cup and tossed it into an empty drum.

❧❧

JJ Bandy, a young laborer from Texas and beer-drinking buddy of Wade's, approached. "Gonna be a hot one, Rembrandt," he said, swabbing the headband of his hard hat with a bandanna. "Whooeee!"

"You're sure of that. I'm trying to plan my day, and the weather is important to me."

"Hot. Bank on it." JJ grinned as he filled a cup. "You see the VIPs?

"Yeah. Who was that?"

"Old man Worth, hisself, and some ass-kissers," said JJ.

"And the vision in the white dress?"

Bandy's quizzical expression made Wade think perhaps he *had* imagined her. He dropped it. They made plans for their usual payday steak dinner at the Lake Texoma Lodge and Wade climbed back down into the hole.

He sang the songs of the day to the staccato accompaniment of the air hammer: "Heartbreak Hotel," "Maybelline," his favorite "Unchained Melody" again and again.

❧❧

Showers, clean T-shirts, clean jeans. JJ and Wade

started most nights with a chicken-fried steak or catfish at
The Sportsman Cafe and coasted into too many beers and
slop eight-ball or shuffleboard afterward at The Spot
Tavern. Madill was situated in the only truly dry county
in Oklahoma, so the beer was 3.2, and no booze, no
"clubs." Wade was saving plenty back for tuition and ex-
penses at the Kansas City Art Institute. Friday nights, JJ
and he would splurge at the new Texoma Lodge motel in
Kingston, and sometimes drive across to the Texas side,
look for girls and never find any.

They usually ended up sitting on the hood of
Wade's '54 Ford in the Madill town square, talking about
their futures, while the locals circled with their radios up
loud. They were both going to be wealthy—JJ in cattle or
oil, Wade as a famous painter.

The Lake Texoma Lodge was mint factory-new
in '58, another tangible result of the postwar boom that
seemed to have no end. Three hundred air-conditioned
rooms, cottages, its own landing strip. The boys passed
the sign that heralded rates $5.00 and up, Fine Food,
Swimming, Boating, Fishing, Golf. A big red boomer-
ang-looking device pointed toward the motel 300 yards
away, the only building in sight on the huge lakefront.

The coffee shop was a precursor to later Dennys and
IHOPs. Chrome banded tables, Naugahyde booths and a
waitress station with order slips on a carousel and a service bell the short order cook would slap. "Three burgers!
BLT nekkid!"

They studied the mimeographed menu backed by imitation leather with cattle brands but nothing listed would sway them from the T-bone steak and baked potato with everything.

She came in for cigarettes. Wade's back was to her in the booth, though he turned to look when he caught JJ's open-mouthed expression. Once more dressed in white, though this time a kind of tennis outfit.

She glanced in their direction and Wade saw that her eyes were gray-green, hair a dark auburn with sun-lightened accents. A swimming pool tan and a figure that would dilate eyeballs. Silver bracelets jangled, no ring that he could see. She paid the cashier and was gone like a light being turned off.

"Be right back," he said to JJ, sliding hurriedly out of the booth.

She had paused outside another, more formal dining room, opened the cigarettes, and was tapping one out. Everyone smoked back then, and they smoked anywhere.

Wade was tongue-tied, but he had to be here. "You like white clothing," he barked inappropriately. *That was unnerving*, he thought. *I've presented myself as a psychopath, or a dope.*

She turned to look at him, a line appearing between her eyes. He could tell she was considering flight. God, she was beautiful.

"I—is something wrong?" she stammered.

"I just—I saw you this morning at the job. In white?

I work there. I wondered why you would be at such a place. And dressed up, you know, in white." *Good god*, he thought, *quit babbling*.

"Not by choice," she said, finger-combing her hair back to reveal earrings with dangling stones that matched her eyes. She seemed to relax, perhaps considering him harmless. "We were flying to Dallas and stopped here. And unless you're a cop, that's all you get."

An imposing fortyish man in golf slacks and polo shirt approached. "There you are, Lily. I looked for you in the dining room—" He took Wade in at a glance.

"Daddy. This is one of your bridge builders. Seems the job is with us wherever we go."

Ignoring Wade's outstretched Zippo, she lit her cigarette with a butane tube that looked like a gold lipstick.

The two men shook hands. Wade was awed. George Worth, himself, second generation owner of Worth Construction. The older man put him at ease, asking him about his job and telling him inside stories about the new safety outfit called OSHA, and the Corps of Engineers monitoring the very work he was doing.

Then he asked Wade to join them for dinner. Wade told him he was with a friend in the coffee shop, another bridge worker. Worth insisted "my boys" join them. Lily rolled her eyes a bit, blew a feather of smoke out of the side of her mouth.

ಌಌಌ

"Appears Lily is violently opposed to flying now, at least in our little Beech Bonanza," Worth explained, as they were seated. "We hit some turbulence. It happens. Anyway, she refuses to go on to Dallas with us and I'm trying to figure out a way to get her safely back home." He turned to her. "Not even a day at Nieman Marcus will get you back in the plane?"

"Not a chance in hell."

"No need to swear, Lily. I have a thought. You all go on ahead and order." Worth dropped his napkin in his chair and left.

JJ was staring at Lily's breasts.

"Stop it," hissed Wade.

JJ arched his eyebrows comically and smiled.

"So, Wade—" She looked at him appraisingly. "— that was you down in that big hole in the ground? You look a lot better cleaned up." She tapped her cigarette on the side of the heavy glass ashtray. "Though you had a certain amount of noble savage appeal. Like James Dean with muscles."

This was going much better now, Wade felt.

"LaWeiner will get a full report on this deal," JJ said out of the side of his mouth, and he snorted. LaWeiner was what he called LaWayne.

⸎

The car was a gleaming black 1956 Lincoln Premiere

convertible with air conditioning. A Worth field car for the Oklahoma job. They had ones just like it on bridge sites in Caracas, Venezuela, Omaha, and Dallas.

The arrangement was simple. Wade had no blemishes on his driving record. His old man was a friend of a Worth VP and his character had been vouched for. Plus, there was the LaWayne scuttlebutt that he might not even like girls. He was to drive Lily to Kansas City, stopping overnight in Tulsa. Wade was to be paid any missed wages plus $100 up front for expenses.

Then he was to return the car to the Lake Texoma Lodge air strip, park it in the Worth hangar, where his car would be waiting. At a certain age, one takes things for granted. This was all so strange to Wade that it actually wasn't. He knew that eventually he'd wake up and none of this would have happened.

Mr. Worth shook his hand and his eyes narrowed slightly. "You seem like a bright boy and I hear good things about you. I don't need to get all paternal and ominous, do I? Remind you of far-reaching consequences?"

"Yes, sir. No, sir."

೮ാ೮ാ

Lily proposed they put the top down after they were out of sight of the lodge. He pulled over into a picnic area with a shaded grove and marveled as the whirring top folded itself neatly behind the back seat.

"Don't look!" she cried, insuring that he would, and she somehow removed her bra from under her sleeveless blouse, then she knotted the blouse ends up under her breasts. She leaned over the seat and opened a bag, fished out some cut-off jeans, said, "Don't look," again, and slid out of her slacks, skinnied into the tight very short jeans, and curled up on the seat, lighting a cigarette. She flipped her cigarette hand toward the windshield, said, "Let's hit the road, Wade."

Wonderful dimples, he thought. Likeable, too, even if she was rich.

ᥱᴈᥱᴈ

She rested her bare feet on the dash, and truckers blasted air horns as they passed, commemorating a fine pair of legs, Wade imagined. He was with them one-hundred percent on that. She swung them around and put her feet in his lap, wiggling them. He corrected the trajectory of the big Lincoln which seemed to be leaving the roadway.

"I'm hungry, Wade." She stretched out "Wade" and made it all sound vaguely salacious.

They idled into the gravel lot of a roadhouse outside of Atoka. Few vehicles were in evidence. A flatbed farm truck with stake sides. A car with different colored fenders and doors. A rusted pickup. Wade wanted cowboy hats for both of them, and pistols. They would take a pocket watch from the proprietor, empty the till, fill a bag with Moon Pies. The Bonnie and Clyde moment passed, but this girl was affecting him.

❦

They played eight-ball at that place, the sunlight slanting in on the green baize tabletop through dusty windows, the locals watching them and drinking beer from bottles. She leaned over the table for a bridge shot and gave the gallery an eyeful. The jukebox played Ernest Tubb, Lefty Frizzell and, once, Dean Martin singing "Memories Are Made Of This," and they danced to that one, all wrapped around one another like the high school prom.

A slim old man in pressed Wranglers and a well-stained Stetson entered. "Whose Lincoln?" he asked the room.

"Ours," Lily said, glancing out the window at it.

"Nice rig," he said.

"It was our wedding present to each other," she said.

That, somehow, pleased the elders, and rounds were bought. A large, weathered woman in a housedress and slippers said "Awww."

Wade was charmed by Lily's ease with the people, sitting at the bar with them, not making fun of anyone, but telling small harmless lies that perpetuated the first one.

They left with a bit of a buzz, promising to send cards, and contemplating a future together. Wade etched the place into his mind for a painting or two.

ﻊﻬﻊﻬ

In McAlester, she said, "Find me a phone."

"If you'll pose for a sketch," he said.

"You bet. Got any change?"

"Nude," he said, as he emptied his pocket. "I'm an artist," he added.

"Okay, but I'd rather you'd wear clothes, at least to draw in," she said sweetly, as she opened the door.

He sat in the car as she talked on the payphone. Her free hand chopped at the air from time to time.

She became agitated, and he heard her say, "Pregnant? You wish, shit for brains!" and she hung the phone up with more force than was needed, three or four times.

They drove in silence for a few miles, pulled in at a Dairy Queen. "So who were you talking to?" he asked casually, after blowing the paper from his straw.

"None of your business." A pause. "My ex-boyfriend."

"Ex as of when?"

"As of that phone call."

"I couldn't help overhearing—"

"You don't want to pursue this." She said it slowly, quietly.

"Pursue what?" he asked innocently. "Want the top up or down?"

"Leave it down." She looked at him, holding an unlit cigarette in one hand, a lighter in the other, her elegantly nailed thumb idly turning the flint wheel. "Are you going to go?"

Wade sat with his back against the door, one arm draped over the steering wheel, the other on the back of the seat. Giving her his best James Dean look, he wished he had worn cowboy boots instead of PF Flyers.

"Are you being someone?" she asked. "Am I to guess?"

He turned to the wheel and started the Lincoln, coloring only slightly.

❧❧❧

"Shoot," said Burdock, leaning across his desk, rolled-out plans held down by rocks and old gears. He tried to feign interest in what LaWayne had on his mind.

"I'm thinkin' a vacation would do me good. You know, get me—"

"Hell, yes, LaWayne. You've earned it. If Wade was here, we'd try him out in your place, but one of your boys can take over. How much time we talkin' about?"

"Week oughta do it."

❧❧❧

Outside Tulsa, top up now, Wade pulled the big Lincoln into a decent-looking motel with a steakhouse across the highway and beer joints scattered about. They discussed going into Tulsa proper and checking into a hotel, but decided to stay where they were. Back from the motel office, he said, "Convention in town, I got the last room, looks like we've got to share."

She blew out a little snort of breath, smiled. "You are full of shit as a ten-pound robin."

"Nice talk," he said, as he waggled two room keys in the air.

"Nice try," she said, snatching a key.

℘℘℘

The restaurant reminded Lily of a steakhouse in Aspen, and that got her started on ski stories, and vacation times, but Wade had little to add since he'd never been on a vacation with his folks, except to his and his sister's grandparents in the summer. Then their folks took off on their own vacations.

Nervously, he'd bought a bottle of vodka at the liquor store outside the restaurant, and pursuant to Oklahoma laws of the time, poured it into "set-ups" of tonic water while they ate and talked. After a few of the vodka tonics, they decided they were having a grand time and became more clever by the minute.

About that time, LaWayne's 1950 Chevrolet limped

into the motel parking lot, steaming and rattling. He pounded the steering wheel until he noticed the company Lincoln parked in front of a room at the other end of the lot. He walked to the motel office and requested a room as close to the Lincoln as he could get.

୧୨୧୨

Lily and Wade walked arm in arm from the restaurant, Wade carrying the fifth of vodka in its paper bag.

"I think you tipped that waitress too much, Wade. I'm a little jealous."

He was overjoyed to hear it. The waitress had flirted with him, and that just made the night even better. They hurried across the highway, and Wade kissed Lily when they reached the other side. It was not a smooth movie kiss—both were unsteady and, by the time they located their mouths, they were filling one another's cheeks with laughter. Neither noticed the 1950 Chevy parked as far away from the Lincoln as the nearly empty lot would allow.

୧୨୧୨

In Lily's room, she said, "Take off your clothes."

"I'm sorry?"

"You said you wanted to paint me in the nude."

"*You* would be nude. But I didn't bring any paints. I

have a sketch pad in my suitcase." Wade took his suitcase to his room, after dropping hers off, brushed his teeth, splashed water on his face, and returned to Lily's room. She wanted to see his sketch book and he allowed her to look at a couple of pages.

"You are really good, Wade." She was engrossed in the book, turning pages slowly, even reverently. "Is this yesterday?" She'd come to the last page and his reconstruction of her standing at the bank of the cofferdam, the light behind her.

"I wanted to draw it before I lost it, you know, before it faded in my mind."

She looked up from the sketch book. "I'll pose for a drawing. But if I don't like it I get to tear it up."

ᡊᢖᡊᢖ

LaWayne sipped a beer in his room. Holding a water glass to the knotty pine wall had revealed only that people were talking in the next room. He couldn't make out what they were saying, just laughter now and then. He'd have to get more aggressive in his detective work if he was going to get anything on Wade and the boss's daughter. The opportunity was immediate and would require action.

He wished he'd thought to bring a camera, but hell, he didn't know how to use one, anyway. This would take bold moves and poker bluffing. He crackled the can in his hand, tossed it in the wastebasket. Wade's goose was as good as cooked.

LaWayne eased his way out the front door, looked both ways, and checked the front window in the room that evidently Wade and the girl were in, though the Lincoln was parked one doorway away from it. Not enough clearance in the curtains to see anything. He stood out in the parking lot, smoking, thinking. Then he strode to his room, and the sliding glass door that opened out to the back and a swimming pool patio, soft drink and ice machines. No one was out there. A woods out back emitted night sounds, and he jumped as the ice machine dumped a crackling new load. The chlorine smell blended with the smell of newly mowed grass.

LaWayne sidled up to the sliding glass door and was pleased to see a crack of light where the curtains weren't pulled shut. He almost choked when the girl walked by in bra and panties and curled up on the bed. He saw Wade settle himself in a chair across from her and it looked like he was drawing her in a large book. Shit-fire, there she was, ready for it and the college boy was making a picture. He heard Wade say, "Technically, that's not nude."

"Use your imagination," she said. She reached for a glass. "I need some more ice."

Wade stood, laid the sketch book in the chair and took her glass.

Oh, shit, thought LaWayne, *he's comin' out to get ice.*

He almost tripped. One of his cowboy boots kicked the door as he turned to run to the privet hedge around the pool and threw himself down behind it. No one came. Wade had used an ice bucket in the room. LaWayne got up, slapped grass clippings from his shirt and jeans with his cowboy hat. Back in place, he now had to take a whiz. He decided to go in the grass by the door while he kept an eye on the girl. This turned out to be problematic as he had a good start on a woody and therefore couldn't pee. He held it in one hand, eyes averted from the girl, hoping it would go down, but he was thinking about her.

"Freeze, you fucking pervert." The voice was ten feet behind him. "Turn around slowly. Slowly. Now. Talkin' to you, bub."

He turned slowly, still holding his penis, which was now quite limp. He was facing the motel night man and a cop. He quickly stuffed it back in his pants, and zipped up, catching it in the zipper. "Eiy yi yi!" he yelled and danced as he unzipped and freed himself.

"Easy there, hoss, quit hoppin' around," the cop said. "Git yourself shot that-a-way."

"That's not him," said the motel night man. "Unless there's a ring of 'em. Fact is, he's a guest, I think."

LaWayne was cuffed and escorted to the patrol car parked in the front lot. Wade and Lily emerged, fully dressed, from their separate rooms, talked to the night manager, who relayed their news to the cop.

"He ain't the peeping tom we've had trouble with,

Officer. He's the feeble-minded cousin of the male guest, Mr. Clover, who's escorting the girl back to KC and the cousin to a home for people like him. He does this all the time, and they apologize. They'll take care of him, and there won't be no more trouble."

They heard the name Worth Construction Company and some "uh-huh"s and "I see"s. And LaWayne was un-cuffed and presented to Wade.

"Keep this jasper inside until you leave, please, sir. We've had some problems around here and he could end up in county lockup," said the policeman. "That could be tough on a person like him."

LaWayne all but growled.

"You bet, sir. I'm sure sorry." Then Wade whispered, but so LaWayne could hear, "He's kind of an embarrass-ment, Officer, but harmless as all getout. Could I get a copy of the police report so I can let the folks at the home know? They should, you know, keep him contained."

"Oh sure. We got all his info. Oklahoma boy. Says he was workin' on a bridge in Madill, but he musta made that up. Just stop in precinct three. They'll be glad to give you a detailed copy." The officer handed Wade a card, shook his head. "Wavin' his johnson around like that, he *should* be in a home."

LaWayne stood, hat in hand, next to Wade, looking down at his boots.

"LaWayne, go to your room. Now," said Wade. "We are going to have us a little talk about your antics."

His lips were compressed as he stifled a laugh. Ol' Bandy was going to eat this up. The police car dipped and bumped onto the highway, throwing some road dust and gravel. The night manager looked at Lily appreciatively, then gave Wade a two finger wave and headed back to his office.

"Night, night, Wade," said Lily.

ↄ⁊ↄↄ

In LaWayne's room, the crackling tension seemed radioactive and rather enjoyable, at least to Wade.

"I want you to know, I wasn't, you know..." said LaWayne, his face turning red.

"Spying? Peeping? Playing with yourself?"

"That last. I wasn't doin' that."

"The evidence would seem to be contradictory," Wade said. "You had your...ah...member in hand when you turned from the window. I believe they called it in-appropriate exposing of oneself in the police report. Weinie waggin' to you."

"I was tryin' ta take a whizz, but, well, anyway, I got to now. Bad."

"Well, go." Wade dismissed him with a flap of his hand, made sure LaWayne heard his puff of annoyed for-bearance.

When LaWayne came out of the bathroom, Wade said, "Way I see it, LaWayne, is you want to be real care-ful back at the job."

"I saw you and her undressed, remember. Her, any-ways. And you was there."

"Hmm. Guess I'll be making copies of that police report. No telling who'd like to see that."

"Okay, okay. I get it." LaWayne seemed in real pain.

"Have a good night's sleep, LaWayne." Wade dug in his jeans pocket for a quarter, flipped it onto the bed. "I understand those Magic Fingers beds are a little bit of heaven. This'll get you ten minutes." He practically skipped from the room. "Enjoy!"

❧❧❧

"Why do you keep promoting that LaWayne guy?" Lily asked, a couple of years into a marriage, for which mutual lust had provided the booster rocket, but true re-spect and conviviality would keep in orbit.

"Well, Lil, he's very good. Plus that old adage, keep your friends close, but your enemies closer. And I actual-ly like the ol' boy."

TEN (MORE) CIRCUMSTANCES BEYOND CONTROL

(1) Bid Letting

He gave me a thick white envelope, nine by twelve, and said, "Carry this wherever you go. Whenever you're out of the truck."

I was mildly puzzled but I didn't question much back then, especially when the boss said it or willed it. He was a mercurial sort. I'd seen him drag an operator physically down off of a D-9 Caterpillar in the field, jump up on it and finish the work himself.

He told me to go to the bid letting in Harney County and be visible. I took a company truck with big logos on the doors, drove around the square a few times, had coffee where the other bidders were. They got quiet when I walked in with my envelope. I sat in a booth and scribbled on it like I was revising numbers. The effect on them was immediate. They huddled and began thumbing through their own papers, changing figures.

I knew what he was doing, making them believe we were low bidders, cutting the pork out of their bids, in cahoots with the town council. At the bid letting, a councilman asked for my bid. I said, "I don't think I'm submitting. My numbers don't add up right."

It was too late for the others to change back, so they went ahead, faces red to various darker shades.

Money was a catalyst for all kinds of violence. I waited for the bid to be won then scooted to the truck and hauled ass. Just past the town sign, a deputy pulled me over. He told me to get out. Then he tore open the envelope, saw it was all blank paper.

He radioed someone. Then he looked at me through silvered aviators a beat too long. "You can go," he said. "Drive safely."

လလ

(2) Transgression

Her tanned skin turned white over her knees as she knelt by the side of the pool. I held onto the tiled ridge, the water lapping about my shoulders.

"Your eyes are red," she said.

"Chlorine. I've been in too long."

I kissed her knee. Briefly. Softly. It seemed natural. She put her hand on my head. It felt like a benediction.

Katherine was born in 1921. I was born in 1943. The year was 1965. It wasn't that she was twice my age. Jesus, she looked like Lana Turner. Heads swiveled wherever she went. More problematic was that she was my mother-in-law.

"I'm going back to the room," she said, pulling her dark glasses down over her eyes. She dropped her lighter, knelt again on one knee. She had a paperback, some lotion, the lighter, her drink. She kept dropping things. Then she scooped them roughly into a straw tote, stood, finished her drink, slopped the ice out onto a grassy area. One piece white suit cut high on the thighs. Legs like a Las Vegas showgirl. I let myself sink back into the pool. I watched her form undulate through the blue water then swim away.

It seemed like the world was on the edge of a cliff. The only reason I wasn't in Vietnam was my 2S classification, married, a kid. Not mine, I'd found out. The draft lottery could still get me. I almost wanted that, if the war hadn't been so futile. Blacks were on a short fuse. Feds were arresting my friends for pot-selling entrapment, and the sentence was medieval. Life was over for them. They were running to Canada. Things were changing. A man had taken pictures of us in Mexico City. I'd noticed the sun on the lens. Then he took off.

ↁↁↁ

(3) Mistaken Identity

I caught glimpses of him. Guy who looked like me, at least dressed like me, blue watch cap, blue ski jacket, Fu Manchu mustache. He drove the same red truck. It felt like a mirror image or someone impersonating me, but why would anyone do that? I was just a guy.

My wife saw this guy pulling a trailer full of hay and a blonde was sitting up against him, she said. "Who's the blonde?" she asked. "You were closer than two coats of paint."

My wife and I had horses then. Could have been me, sure enough, but it wasn't. I told her there was a guy who looked like me, running around.

"How convenient," she said.

Then, in a bar in town, George, he was the owner, said, "Boy, are you in trouble." He plunked a beer down in front of me.

"Oh?"

"Yeah, you musta been drunk."

"What are you talking about?"

"What you yelled at Dunny Osborne's wife."

Dunny was a known badass in town. I didn't run with him. His wife was hot.

"I didn't yell anything at her."

"She said it was you, your truck."

Then my wife saw the guy up close at the Dairy Queen. "I half believe you, now," she said. "He does look like you. And his truck's the same. He asked me if I'd like to take a shower with him."

"What'd you say?"

"Nothing. I left. But I got his license number."

George told me he came into the bar with another guy, and he had both arms in casts, held out from his body by supports. I wondered how he took a leak. George moved around all stiff like Frankenstein, and was able to reach his zipper.

"Said he had a dirt bike accident. Bet it was a Dunny accident."

಄಄಄

(4) Karma

He did three tours and called it quits. Wounded, he was going to get a desk job he didn't want. A captain when he hung it up.

He disappeared up in the Sierras, came down for supplies, had a beater of a Land Cruiser he kept somewhere by a snow gate. Drove it into Fresno for supplies, a woman, who knew? A meth punk tried to jack it from him down there. He wasn't buying it. The freak shot him in the face.

Three tours, wounded twice, came out fairly whole, and a garbage bag did him in. So, if you paid taxes, you paid for this freak for however long—his meals, his meds, his TV, his weights if he wants to use them. Go figure.

Anyways. Rudy Teale. Captain A. Rudolph Teale.

Before his untimely death, he was up in the Sierras panning for gold over on the Yuba, and he ran into some Hells Angels.

They took an interest in this gold business and asked him to show them how to do it. He showed them what it took and how much work it was for a little nothing smidgen of gold flake, but there was always the chance of a nugget somewhere. They didn't mind work, so they all lined up on the Yuba, running cold with trout back-pedaling and idling in the pools.

All told, they got about eleven bucks worth of gold in a week, laughed, and said, "Screw this, look us up in Fresno, Rudy," and they were off in a showy blast of drag pipes and skittery back wheels.

Karma. Don't ever doubt it. Two of them ended up where the meth douche was. He was bragging about taking down a marine captain. They perked up, shanked this fool while they told him why. I'm just sayin'.

e⁄ɔℇ⁄ɔ

(5) Blue Dress

Steel, glass, trees. A corporate woods. My father offices here and I am dropping in, unannounced, to touch base, as he says.

"Come anytime," he says.

I am on a pleasant bridge that crosses a creek from where I've parked. The openings through the tunnel of trees allows the sun to sprinkle the walkway with shifting patterns of gold and fawn.

She appears on the level above mine. I pause and watch her approach the building. She is in her twenties, my age, stunning in a shimmery electric blue dress, the breeze toying with her skirt. She walks with purpose. Lustrous black hair, slim long legs, olive luminous skin— she looks like a model. She raises her right arm, straight out, palm up, then she closes her palm into a fist, draws it toward her.

It is a curious gesture, intimate. I take it to mean I have you by the balls, you in the building.

My father emerges, smiling. They embrace. My mother, with her menopausal episodes and drinking, is no match for this vision in a blue dress. I understand, but that's far from approval. I step back, unseen.

The sun flashes off his glasses and his smile is warm.

∽∾∽∾

When I do get to know her, I see her skin, though luminous, is prone to acne. She sits cross-legged in a T-shirt, watching Saturday morning cartoons, warm beer between her thighs. How does she explain the hickeys to him?

She has long conversations with Keith in Los Angeles on her iPhone. "He is a hair stylist," she says. "To the
red carpet celebrities. A dear, dear friend."

He will put her up when she goes back out there to
model again.

"I'd like you to meet my father," I say. "Maybe
lunch today?"

ৡৡ

(6) Hardball

It was spring, 1963. JFK's last year. The Rizzutto kid
was fourteen. He beaned a pinch-hitter in a little league
game, hardball. The ball caught the batter below his helmet and he died after a short coma. It was unintentional.
Kids don't have the control they need sometimes. That
was on Wednesday.

Mike, the pitcher, lived across the hall from our
apartment. He was a polite, handsome kid, an ath-
lete/scholar with life stretched out in front of him, marred
now, but we hoped he'd get past it.

About a week before, my wife's old man had given
us tickets to the Shrine Circus for Friday night. I meant to
give them away, but forgot, and Frannie suggested we
take Mike and his brother and sisters to the circus, maybe
get his mind off the tragedy.

The circus was the last place I wanted to be on a Friday night, but I agreed. Mike's folks were grateful, if distracted.

We sat on a bleacher row about halfway up. Mike seemed to be getting into it, relaxing, shushing his sisters. The acts were pretty good, actually. Yetta Wallenda was atop a very tall fiberglass pole making it whirl in ever-widening arcs. I was aware of the Wallenda tragedies so was sure this pole act was safer than ever.

When she fell, I knew it was part of the act. I smiled, probably quizzically, as the spotlight followed her down, wondering how she'd resolve this apparent fall into a miraculous recovery. Then she hit a guy wire on her back, spun, and hit the sawdust with a thud, face down. The spotlight lit her up in a big circle.

Fran said, "Turn off the fucking light," through gritted teeth.

I gaped. We herded the kids out.

I'd like to think I imparted wisdom beyond my twenty some odd years to Mike at that point, but I don't even remember talking to him. I don't even recall depositing the kids at their home. I probably just made a stiff drink when I got home, which was my way with things out of my control. The trouble with that is, just about everything is out of my control.

Mike was fifteen when JFK was assassinated later that year. He saw Oswald killed on national TV two days later.

✌✌

(7) High Bridge

He was scared shitless, up this high. But he was more scared not to come up—off balance with the bucket of bolts, a drift pin, and a spud wrench. The steelworkers above him placed angle-iron sides and he put the cross pieces on, an X, stuck the drift pin in a hole to secure it while he bolted the open holes. Then he'd tap the pin out, bolt that hole. Three-inch angle iron was his footing. Climb up the X, do another one. No one used harnesses. It never occurred to him. OSHA was not a factor in the 1950s.

He'd heard about steeplejacks and mountain climbers just letting go, relaxing backward to gravity, falling without a sound, no yelling. It was a rapture of some sort, a fuck you to fear. They gave themselves to the monster.

The wind was wilder up here. His hard hat blew off. He grabbed for it reflexively and lost his footing for an instant before he hooked an elbow on the X, hugging it while he watched the metal hat fall. The hard hat turned over and over in seeming slow motion as it fell, smaller and smaller. He saw it hit the deck a hundred feet below, a hundred and fifty, bounce off the plate steel, into the water, flashing in the sun. A couple of men tying steel below looked up, shading their eyes.

He left his bucket hooked to the X, climbed down X by X, slowly, shaking. When he got to the bottom, he fell forward on all fours. He saw the foreman's Red Wing boots, heard his voice, lowered so only he could hear, "You don't like working high, you don't have to, son. Hell, I got welders who won't get up on a stepladder."

ᕽᕽᕽ

(8) 1949

"It's not 'stoopid,' stupid, it's stupid."

The Atomic Bomb Guy pronounced it 'ste-yoo-pid" in his British accent. He was Pete's stepfather, born in London. It was August, 1949 and the Atomic Bomb Guy was drunk. He always got drunk around the anniversary of Hiroshima. Pete had found the plaque somewhere in the dusty basement of the Tulsa house that listed his step-father's name with those of twenty-one others who had been essential in some design that helped make the atom-ic bomb, a switch or something. His stepfather wouldn't elaborate.

Pete had just said he thought it was stupid that he couldn't have a Red Ryder BB gun when everyone else in the neighborhood had one. "I'm twelve," he said.

The Atomic Bomb Guy slurred when he said, "Save your stupid allowance instead of spending it on stupid crap and buy the stupid fucking thing."

"Okay, I stoopid fucking will," Pete said.

And they both laughed. Atomic poured himself some bourbon, poured Pete some more beer in an orange juice glass. Pete didn't like the taste much but he liked the feeling it gave him. "I mean stee-yoooo-pid," he said, and laughed, belched, and laughed some more. This was fun.

"Here," Atomic said, handing Pete a five dollar bill. "Go get the stupid thing."

Pete's head swam as he pulled his bicycle up from the lawn and squinted against the sun. He knew the BB gun was three seventy-five at the hardware store. He'd have money left over. He wobbled out into the street, got control of his bike, pedaled hard as he rounded the corner, leaning into it. A car honked as he sped through the intersection. He yelled "Stee-yoo-pid!" over his shoulder, skidding to a flamboyant stop at the store, leaving a black mark on the sidewalk.

ᥱᕽᥱᕽ

(9) Street Fight

The old Chevy vapor-locked again. Butch pulled over to the curb, somewhere in east KC, not a good place to break down, for Southwest High School guys. The enmity with Central High went way back. His two friends, Maury and Duane got out when he lifted the hood.

"It'll start when it cools off," Butch said.

"I hear if you wrap the fuel line in tinfoil, it won't vapor lock," said Duane.

A loud car pulled up alongside, a lowered '48 Mercury. Three guys inside. One closest to them said, "Get that piece a shit off the road."

"Fuck you," said Butch.

The three scrambled out of the Mercury. Butch told Maury and Duane to get in, quick, and slammed the hood down. One of the approaching three had his hand in the way and the hood caught it and bounced. The guy grabbed his hand and whirled away from the car, shrieking.

Butch was in the car now but saw that one of the assailants was going to punch him through the open window. He opened the door and the boy swung his fist hard into the edge of it.

The attacker clutched his hand to his chest and bent double with pain.

The third boy was on the other side of the car running at Duane but didn't see the fireplug in his way. Duane shut the door and the boy hit the fireplug, crotch high, and went down holding himself, moaning.

The car started. They burned rubber pulling out. In the rearview mirror, Butch saw a police car pulling up to the abandoned Mercury which was parked out in the street blocking traffic.

He turned left, then right, then left again, and headed for home.

The story was they'd won a fight with hated rivals.

☙❧☙

(10) Blue Moon

They had no prenuptial agreement—it was love, or something that seemed intense enough to pass for it. He was fifty, she was twenty-eight. Hunter was now fifty-three and, in the intervening years, had seen enough corrosion and killing moments to last him.

"I want the house," Meghan stated, looking over his shoulder as though talking to someone behind him.

He used to look around behind him, but no one was ever there.

"It's expensive," he said. "You sure?"

"My lawyer is and that's good enough for me."

The house in question was a postmodern glass and cor-ten steel beach house in Malibu facing the ocean. He'd just spent forty-seven grand on a failed hardscaping deal in front of it, the side facing the street, that featured waterfalls, a huge fiberglass boulder and a reflecting pool that needed constant attention. A phony guy in a turban and an accent that seemed Chechen at times, or bad British at others, dreamed it up with Meghan. Hunter suspected they did a lot of pot in the process.

"My job's in trouble," he said, as though to himself.

"Tell somebody who gives a shit." She shrugged and turned to check her phone for whatever she checked on it. Perhaps a sext from Mr. Moon.

"I will," he mused. "I'll find that person or persons, and run it by them."

He could kill her right now. Cut glass ashtray. Bonk! Get Mr. Moonbeam, or whatever his dumbass title was, to open up the fake boulder in front. Ramon Rising Moon. His real name was probably Wayne or Lenny or something. Jones. Rabbinowitz. Ramon Rising Moon had had the boulder made out of fiberglass and it was already cracking, pulling apart fibrously.

It looked like an alien egg on a bad movie set. And the reflecting pool leaked. Ramon had suggested a blue pool liner. He'd get Ramon to open the egg, then use the same cut glass ashtray on him, inter them both, have a body shop come by and repair the boulder. Or learn fiberglassing himself. Might come in handy when the agency fired his ass. A major car account was slipping through his fingers.

She was crying, though still swiping at her phone with a two-fingered gesture that apparently made it do things on the screen.

He almost laughed. It looked like she was trying to grasp something behind the screen. Like a child trying to pick up a jelly bean under glass.

LA 1st Daily headline: Adman's ex-wife and shady contractor disappear. He says they both got "what they deserve: each other." Beach house for sale. "I can't afford the damn thing now. It's hers, anyway. Looks like it will be up for taxes in November if they don't come back from Belize. I shut off the credit cards." Is this her?

(ATM pic in Carmel) Or did Person of Interest hubby hire a lookalike? <u>Read more.</u>

THE HOLE IN THE CEILING
AT THE REFUGE TAVERN

The wildlife refuge in southeast Kansas is actually five hundred refuges and about 7,000 acres with the Marais Des Cygne River snaking through the approximate middle of it. A Kansas City lawman, who had to search for an escapee from justice in the refuge, said more weird shit goes on in there than in the Amazon basin. "People live in there like blow-dart tribes, but they have a hell of a lot more weapons options. I wouldn't be surprised to find rocket launchers in there. Jack-pine savages."

Tall, long-legged, moving deliberately, carrying one of the heavy PVC container tubes across his arms like a piece of firewood. Cobb *strode*, he didn't walk. Seven league boots. God, what would the world be if Cobb got old? Travis thought. Cobb wasn't young, maybe sixty, but he looked younger than his years, a boyish shock of salt-and-pepper hair hanging over one eye, a two-day beard on a grin-ready face. Travis played the Cobb game in his head, the game that he and Breeze had cooked up so many years ago when they were kids.

If Cobb was a car, he'd be a super-blown 454 Trans-Am with racing slicks, the color of red-hots and no mufflers at all, fire coming outa the headers. If Cobb was…what, a song?…he'd be "Folsom Prison Blues" by Johnny Cash *and* Merle *and* Lefty Frizzell, all at once with Chuck Berry on guitar and that Led Zeppelin guy on drums. The Cobb game got so wild, so over the top, that Breeze and Travis would yell over each other's descriptions and crazy Cobbisms until they would fall down in high-pitched laughing heaps, almost peeing their pants.

Cobb. He moved in *gusts*, nothing in his way when he was on his road, accomplishing, getting things done. Not skinny, but no fat on him, with ropy-veined thick forearms, feet in Red Wing workboots, they said when he was a field superintendent on the bridge jobs in Managua and Rio and Texas, that he ate standing up and shit a-walking. Travis always felt pride that Cobb was blood. Even now with his uncle on crank, it was just a fact, a "deal with it" kind of thing. He was on it because of Vinita's senility, the pain of her moving beyond his help, beyond his protection. It was pain medication, and if anyone had a problem with it, fuck 'em.

When she wasn't having "spells," he tried hard to

stay away from it. He'd get off it. Travis knew it was temporary. Cobb felt addictions were for people who couldn't deal with life straight on. But he was bewildered about Vinita. He couldn't get his big arms around that one, his wife shorting out like that.

Travis took the last PVC container of LaCygne Green marijuana they'd packed, followed Cobb, emulating his walk like a kid would do, snorting with a little blow of secret laughter at that picture, long strides, watch out, Cobb coming. "One fist of iron, the other of steel, if the left one don't getcha, then the right one *weel.*"

He thought back to when his old man was around, before the big C killed him. Reno Pete, they called him. He was Cobb's older brother and Cobb idolized him. Cobb and Reno, man. Travis had actually learned to be a little scared for people who crossed them. Even bad people. Cobb and Reno Pete were a natural disaster if you got their attention in the wrong way.

One of the Hoover boys accosted Travis's mother in Self's Refuge Tavern near the turnoff to the St. Cyr compound. Travis and his mother were waiting for Reno to pick them up, after she'd met Travis at the school bus on the last day of school, and drive them home. Hoovers were mean-bad and you just didn't ever mess with them, but even the head Hoover, the old man, Perf, would have told that one, leave that woman alone, that's Reno Pete's old lady, that's a death wish, boy.

Perf Hoover's full name was Perfect Venus Hoover

and they say that's how he got so mean, all the fights over his name. No one ever laughed at his name after he'd turned about fifteen, except a deputy sheriff in Fulton, Missouri. Perf had done time in Jeff City over that one. Manslaughter.

Travis recalled his anger and his helplessness when North Hoover—he had brothers named East, West, South, among others—had tried to get his mother to dance and hurt her arm jerking her out of her chair, spilling her 7-Up.

"Leave her alone," Travis had shouted, throwing his ten-year-old body at North Hoover, smelling the man's acrid sweat-and-sawdust-mixed-with-booze aroma on his rough denim work clothes. Hoover smacked him aside, into a clatter of chairs and empty tables. Travis had a ringing in his ears, then he heard Hoover say it.

"She don't want to be left alone, showin' her tits like that in a T-shirt, her ass hangin' out a shorts. Fuck off, boy."

"Hey, North," said one of the brothers. "Leave off. Them are St. Cyrs."

The barmaid came to the table and said, quietly, "You best leave, hon, they're drunk."

Then she helped Travis up. Travis shook her off and he and his mom left, Travis glaring over his shoulder at the Hoovers, his mother holding back tears until they'd gotten to the road.

North made an obscene gesture with his mouth and

waggling tongue at Travis's mother from the doorway.

Travis wanted to go back in, but she held his arm tight, talking through clenched teeth, "No. *No*. You will stay with me. And we won't say a word to your father, you hear me? Not a word. It's over."

His anger was such that a blood mist clouded his eyes and seeped through his thinking. He knew, at ten, what it meant to see red.

It got out. News in the wildlife refuge seemed to travel with the wind. Reno and Cobb acted nonchalant about it at home. But they left together, Cobb with the sawed-off twelve gauge. Travis saw him pull it out from the beam above the fireplace in its soft, oiled wrap. Cobb dropped some shells in the pockets of his cutoff work shirt.

Days later, Travis got the story from Breeze, who'd heard it from the older boys. Cobb and Reno had entered the bar. Cobb, with the shotgun at waist level, advised patrons that anyone who wanted to leave should do it pretty quick. Chairs scooted on the board floor and barstools whirled. There weren't many there, other than three Hoovers and a couple of their friends. The few others headed out, throwing gravel in the parking lot. The owner, Bert Self, was told to sit down, hands on a table, if you please.

Reno walked over to North, who jumped up and swung at him. Reno blocked it and punched him in the Adam's apple. The others started to move but Cobb said,

"This is him and North, boys. I got number five birdshot in here and I *will* pull the trigger. It don't make a shit to me."

Reno had decked North. Then he picked the man up by the belt and shirt collar, and, with an animal sound, he ran and whirled, like those Scottish pole-throwers, and flung Hoover up into the lowered ceiling tiles.

The hole was there for years.

It wasn't physically possible. Hoover was maybe a mean, scrapping 175 lbs. Reno Pete was not as tall as Cobb but about 185 and just under six foot, arms like tree stumps, but not enough heft to throw a man like he surely did. Bert Self saw it ringside and sober, and he told it about the same every time.

When Hoover landed, they thought he was dead. Reno Pete, owing to his Vietnam habits and French ancestry they said, pulled a small-but-much-sharpened bone-handled pocketknife from his jeans pocket, snicked it open deftly, and cut off the bottom half of Hoover's left ear, wrapped it in a bandanna.

"Ears bleed, looks worse than it is," he said. "I'd have taken it all but I want him to be able to hear me comin'." Then he smiled, still breathing heavy, nodded to Self, said, "We'll talk about the damages."

Self, looking straight ahead, just fluttered one hand off the table, waved him away.

Reno walked out the door. Cobb backed out after him.

The hole in the ceiling tiles and the torn aluminum frames were eyed by many over the years, as they gazed up into the darkness beyond, thinking about powerfully focused anger. Another page in the St. Cyr legend.

That was when Travis began to fight in school. And when his mother died, it was hell on wheels.

A bully once told him, "You think you're bad don't you?"

His answer was, "So bad that I'm going to make you look good."

And he did. He became a bully-hunter. If he couldn't beat them fair and square, he stalked them until he got them alone and clubbed them. Cobb got him started in a boxing program at the Salvation Army gym in town, so he'd at least know what the rules were, maybe channel the anger. Travis took it into high school to Golden Gloves, and then to college boxing. He was a slugger, a mauler, not artful. He quit boxing when he quit college.

Cobb grew the LaCygne Green all around the compound, but never in a linear, cultivated look. He grew it in the horseweed, along the fence lines, in clumps where the peat rot looked good around old logs. Places where the planes could never see it. He claimed it was number two in the world. A book said so. Breeze and Travis drove it to Arizona and New Mexico in trailer-loads of brome hay. From there, some of it even went to Mexico.

They placed the tubes of LaCygne Green into a grave-sized hole, along with the others. Travis laid two-by-fours across them, anchored to the sides, to take the weight of the dirt, and Cobb started the backhoe.

When they drove up to Self's Refuge Tavern, Travis waited while his uncle spit out the rest of his chew, hiked his jeans.

"Let's go kill some a them pesky-ass brain cells," Cobb said, moving his fists in a way that always made Travis laugh. He claimed college had ruined Travis, made him too smart. When he opened the door to Self's, Travis felt the cold air meet the barrier of humidity and heat of the day.

The place was dark and empty. One of the Self kids was tending bar. Joe, the quiet one. The TV was on, a KC Royals game, Travis noted. June and it looked like they might finally get a shot if their bats stayed hot and the pitching didn't fall off.

"Cobb, Travis," Joe said, swiping a damp rag on the bar in front of them, placing two coasters. Joe would end up owning the place, thought Travis. He was the hardest working of the bunch.

Cobb said, "Extra cold draw beer and a shot for everyone in this tin horn, Mayberry, two-bit, backwoods outfit."

Joe smiled as much as he ever did, which was a slight broadening of his mouth on one side. "That include the vehicle that just pulled up?"

They looked out the storefront window to the parking lot. A black Range Rover was sitting in its own settling dust. Both front doors opened and a bearded young man emerged from the driver side, looked around, removed his sunglasses, and hung them from the neck of his T-shirt. A slender brunette girl stepped out from the passenger side, stretched, arching her back, then bent forward, and touched the toes of her running shoes. She was dressed in short shorts, a crop-top T-shirt, sunglasses back on top of her head.

"Why not?" said Cobb. "Ask 'em what they want. Don't look like beer-and-shot folks."

When they entered, they looked around, allowing their eyes to adjust to the dark cavernous room. Travis watched the girl.

Cobb paid them no attention at all. The young man seemed nervous, kinetic, while the girl was almost languorous, a lazy smile appearing on her face as she took in Cobb and Travis.

The man approached the bar and spun a coin on it, then said, "Tonic and ice." Then he turned to the girl, "Name yer pizen, podnuh."

A flash of annoyance crossed her smooth face, was gone like a soft flicker of summer lightning. She licked her lips and sat on a barstool near Cobb. "Boulevard Pale Ale," she said.

"No tonic, no Boulevard, sorry," Joe said. "Them's the beers, on the sign." He thumbed over his shoulder.

Travis liked Boulevard Beer. The wheat beer was his favorite at KU. He felt like telling the girl, but that would be like saying, "Hi, I went to college, we're not all hicks here."

The man grinned, sighed, said, "Seven-Up and ice. Oh wait. You have Seven-Up? You have ice?"

"You're in luck on both a them choices," Joe said.

The girl had a Bud Lite.

"It's on the handsome gent in the cutoff sweatshirt," Joe said, nodding at Cobb.

They raised their drinks to him. Cobb nodded and smiled.

Everyone was quiet for a minute, then the young guy with the beard said, "One of you is supposed to ask, 'what brings you young folks to our part of the world?' That's how my movie starts, anyway."

"You lost or what?" Joe said.

That caught the girl in mid swallow and she choked out a little laugh.

"My GPS says we're at the very doorway of the Marais DesCygne Wildlife Refuge, where we mean to go look around. We're photographers. I am, anyway. She's studying under me." He beamed at the girl. "Learning anything? Under me?"

"Lots. Mostly 'don't be that guy.'"

"Pictures of what?" Cobb said, watching the girl.

"Pictures of her naked, running with the herons," said the photographer.

"Kind of thorny in there for running around naked," Travis said, "and the herons are shy."

He noticed her necklace. It was a fine chain with a silver pendant of a fairy that ended in a little spoon— coke spoon.

"Would you gentlemen guide us? For a fee, of course. Hey I should introduce us," The guy stood up and was suddenly between Cobb and Travis in the small space between the stools. He placed a hand loosely on each of their shoulders. Cobb shook it off and turned on his stool to face the photographer. The guy backed off and gave them each a card. "Gareth Gilmore. Call me Gary. And that—" He paused, turning to the girl, "—is Hayley. Call her...umm...anything. Say, I'd love to shoot you guys and Hayley, she could wear like a formal gown, or a little black dress, both of which we have, and you two are perfect the way you are. See? We go back in the swamp, or whatever that is in there, and just start shooting. Next thing you know we're in the slick pubs. Sound good?"

Cobb looked at Travis. "I think we'd better guide them, you know?"

"Yeah. Like away from certain dangerous areas."

"Goody!" Gary said, causing Cobb to slide a look at Travis. "How much?"

"Well, if we just go for an hour or so, no charge," Cobb said. "But no pictures of us, hear? Just ol' Hayley there, with the occasional heron or whatever turns up."

The girl looked at Cobb and upended the bottle, lips around the end of it, still looking sideways at him, neck arched.

Gary did a sort of moonwalk to the jukebox, whirled, and dug for change. The girl turned on her barstool, watching him with a smile. "Gary can be very amusing," she said to Cobb.

She slouched, back against the bar, elbows on the bar in back of her. There was no way she could look bad, Travis noted.

"Take your word for it," said Cobb.

He tossed his shot down, drank some beer as the introductory strains of "Jesus, Take The Wheel" began to play. Gary danced out of synch to it in a parody of hip hop, his hands often at his crotch, grinning crazily at Hayley. He wore a sort of safari-looking vest with pockets full of apparently heavy items which slapped and thumped about as he danced. He then snapped his fingers and, lowering his head with his hands high in the air, he performed a Flamenco dance, stomping his heels.

"Fucking awesome," said Hayley, smiling in her own world.

ᘓᘓᘓ

Outside, Gary insisted they ride together in the Range Rover but Cobb and Travis climbed into their truck and led the way.

"Why not ride with them?" asked Travis

"You're welcome to, though I wouldn't recommend it," said Cobb. "Them two are not as squirrelly as they act. They're as bad as they get, though."

"I get a definite pelvic sensation from her."

Cobb laughed. "You and Breeze, hound dogs to the core."

"Admit it, Cobb, she's hot."

Cobb just shook his head, took a swig from the beer bottle between his legs. He signaled a turn and pulled into one of the more touristy entrances to the wildlife refuge, a hard gravel road that ran parallel to the Marais DesCygne River. "We'll take 'em plenty far away from the goods, maybe by the sign painter's shack." He turned again, down a dirt road that wound through a cut with canyon-like sides, into a dark canopy of old growth trees. The road led to an open meadow with what was left of the sign painter's house and outbuildings.

The sign painter was long dead, but his ramshackle buildings were still there, falling in on themselves. Many of his hand-painted signs had been stolen by folk-art hunters but since the land had been posted, some still survived. Most of the signs had proclaimed *The End* in incomprehensible, though biblical-sounding, ramblings— while others ranted at *The Federale Guverment*. Some were curses on anyone entering. Some were aimed at for- nicating youth. The sign painter had used a lot of black and white paint, and energy, but not on his buildings. The signs were nailed anywhere that would hold them: trees, fences, barn sides. The gray, deeply weather-etched wood of the chicken coop still stood, only due to the signs that held it up. Cobb pulled up alongside a skeletal rusting

squeeze chute, once used for doctoring livestock. A barely legible sign on the leaning fence said, *the gret Whore
sits inthrone over manny waters, the Whore kings of the
earth have gone whorng with. Revolatoin 17.*

Gary slammed the Range Rover door, said to Hayley,
"Oh, man, get a load of this shit. This is wonderful! Get
my Hasselblad, oh, man. Go stand by that whore sign.
Whoa!"

The motor drive of the expensive camera whirred
and clicked. Gary posed her topless, then nude by the
sign. Cobb watched, expressionless, drinking his beer.
Travis was conscious that his mouth was open and closed
it with a little pop from his lips. He held his beer bottle
loosely by the neck at his side. Cobb winked at him.
"Shed them knickers purty quick, didn't she?" he said out
of the side of his mouth.

Travis saw that her pubic hair was shaved into a
careful sort of mohawk look.

"Get that little black sequin number, and heels. Hurry. The light, it's perfect!"

She wriggled into a short black cocktail dress by the
open door of the Range Rover, and shook it down over
her, fooled around behind her back with the zipper, then
called to Travis, "Zip me?"

He marched right over and zipped her up. She put
one hand on his shoulder for balance as she put the shoes
on, and a charge, not unlike voltage, ran through him. She
then stood by the sign in some quite provocative poses,

her face more animated than Travis had seen since she arrived. Then she was once more dormant, but still, in her dress and pose, somewhat threatening just by dint of her deadpan look. Gary placed the camera on the ground, started moving about with a digital camera, checking the small screen on the back from time to time. He rushed to the SUV and pulled out a pump shotgun, which he handed her. Travis noted that Cobb tensed up at this development, but then Gary just kept on shooting as she held the gun in a number of different ways. The combination of odd light on her sequined dress, the sign, and her poses caused Travis to shiver involuntarily. This whole deal was damned weird, he decided.

"Couldn't get you to stand in back of her, could I?" Gary said to Travis. "Sort of put your arms around her?"

"No faces," said Cobb.

"His whole face will be in shadow. I'll show you on the screen."

Cobb nodded. Travis hitched up his jeans, walked to her and stood behind her.

"Camera-shy. You a fugitive?" she asked him as he held her loosely.

"Nope. You?"

"Yeah." She backed into him. "From certain things. Not justice. Not yet."

"Now you," said Gary. "Cobb, is it? Stand over here with the shotgun, take her by the hair."

"Nah, we're done. You all are on your own now. We

got chores." Cobb moved toward the pickup. Travis hesitated, but started after him, slowly. He turned, gave a half
wave to the girl, and noticed that Gary was depositing red
shells into the shotgun. He swallowed hard. "Cobb?"

"Chores huh. Slop the pigs? Plow the forty? That'll
wait, Cobb." Gary drew the name out like he thought it
was funny. He was half aiming the shotgun, now. "For
now, we got us another chore, Cobbman. Cobbomeister.
Take us to your backhoe."

Cobb stood, watching Gary, arms at his sides, thinking. Travis looked at the girl who was skinnying into her
shorts and tennis shoes. She balled up the cocktail dress
and shoes, tossed them into the Range Rover.

"Oh come on, don't act dumber than you are. We
watched you bury the shit. Now we need you to dig it up.
One of the few things I don't do is operate machinery.
Bet I could, though, if I had to shoot you both. How hard
could it be?"

℘℘℘

Travis drove, Cobb sat in the passenger seat of the
Range Rover. Gary and Hayley sat well in the back rather
than right behind them. Gary rested the shotgun on the
seatback of the empty seat behind Travis and Cobb.

"Sixteen gauge," Gary said. "What gauge did you
have when you covered your bro, the day he threw that
guy through the ceiling at that bar? Oh, yeah, we know

all about you guys. Did our homework. Especially on LaCygne Green. It's already sold. All we do is deliver it and, boom, payday."

Travis was stumped. He couldn't wreck the vehicle. That might not hurt the right people. No way to grab the barrel of the gun. He was pretty sure they'd be killed once the tubes were dug up. Gary and Hayley were real bad, he was sure of it. Maybe even thrilled by the prospect of doing them in. And the police would treat it as a drug killing, go after some Mexicans who had tried to muscle Cobb once before. Joe would turn them on to this pair, but they might be long gone before anyone found Travis and Cobb. He cut a look at Cobb, whose forehead showed a series of lines, and he seemed to be chewing on the inside of his mouth. None of this was reassuring to Travis. His uncle was a ranger. Didn't rangers have various escapes up their sleeve, levitation perhaps?

Gary was going on to Hayley about the ceiling incident: "It was like the Hatfields and McCoys. Reno Pete cut the other guy's ear off, after he threw him. You can't make this shit up, I mean it. Say, Cobbo, how come this didn't start like a big range war? Hmm?"

"The Hoovers met and decided it was North Hoover's fault was all," Cobb said, reasonably enough.

"How civilized. Wow, like a family council, you mean?"

"Yes, like that."

"Hayley, mark this, it's...like history, it's like very

real, you know, salt of the earth people, noble though tacky, resolving their difficulties without interference from, like, the *revenooers*." Gary started laughing, more like giggling.

Hayley joined him. "Don't, Gary, I'm going to pee my shorts, quit."

They were re-exploding with giggles like demented children. *Jesus*, thought Travis, *we're fucking dead meat*, as he pulled up in the clearing where the backhoe sat, framed by vines, sunflowers, and a dramatic stack of cumulus clouds.

"Kamatsu," Gary said. "Have you no patriotism? What's wrong with good old American iron? You're in a Red State here, Cobber."

"Be ready," Cobb said, low.

"Mm-hmm." *Okay*, thought Travis. *For what? But yes, I was fucking born ready. And Cobb is, was, after all, a ranger.*

"Fire that fucker up," Gary said. "Either one of you."

Cobb strode to the backhoe. *Strode, like he does everything*, thought Travis, *with purpose*. With a by-god-work-to-do forward lean. Travis knew there wasn't a gun in the Kamatsu. You just didn't leave firearms laying around in the refuge. They had a way of disappearing. So did backhoes, as a matter of fact, but they'd planned to haul this one home tonight.

Cobb had drop guns here and there, but not while doing everyday chores. Maybe, just maybe, he had a boot gun, because they'd been moving LaCygne Green. The 30-30 lever action was behind the seat in the pickup.

Black smoke rolled out of the exhaust, then cleared. Travis could smell the diesel.

Cobb extended the boom out, out. What was he doing? The bucket was low to the ground and the boom was almost straight. The tracks were lifting off the ground in back. Gary looked puzzled and raised the shotgun. Then the boom swung all the way around in a shrieking half circle, lifting one set of tracks off the ground, the bucket flying around barely above the dirt. It caught Gary with a sickening thud and the shotgun went off wild. The girl ran for the Range Rover, but Travis had the keys. If nothing else, before he was killed, he planned to drop them into the brush.

The backhoe rocked as Cobb released the clutch for the bucket and it hit the ground, stabilizing the machine. Gary was under the toothed bucket. Hayley now ran toward the gun. Travis beat the girl to the shotgun, held it muzzle in the air.

Cobb raised the boom, shook Gary off of the bucket, and he fell like chunks of Kansas clay. The backhoe rocked and clanked but nothing like the wild, seemingly impossible circumscription of moments before.

Travis already knew this couldn't follow a legal path of any sort. Police involvement was out of the question. All would do time, nobody unscathed. Might even be murder charges on Gary. After all, who knew for sure he wouldn't have killed them? Travis sighed, tried to breathe deeply, but he was shaking now from an overdose of adrenaline, his breath coming shallow.

Cobb climbed down off the track of the now quiet machine. He glanced once at Gary's remains, walked to Travis and the girl.

"Didn't know if I'd get him or not," he said, disregarding the girl altogether. "We'll part that vehicle out in Kansas City," he mused, as if to himself.

The girl let out a mewing sound. *She looked feral*, Travis thought, *her eyes darting*. She seemed to shrink into herself. Then she bolted. She ran crazily toward the river and the underbrush. Cobb turned slowly to watch her run, thumbs hooked in his pockets. He spit on the ground. Still had his Red Man chew, Travis noted.

"What do we do?" said Travis.

"She's running right at the dropoff," Cobb said.

Travis imagined her breaking through the brush, legs bicycling in the air as gravity took over. Thirty foot cut where the Marais Des Cygne river turned back on itself, then shot a whitewater mass southeast in the rainy season. It was way down now but the deep current was still swift.

"Take the Range Rover to the sandbar. She'll come up there. If she got to the water. Wait one, I'll check." Cobb strode to the dropoff.

WINCHESTER TATTOO

I only had two horses left. I told myself they were a sculpture reference. I did life-sized horses in welded steel, some smaller ones in bronze. I no longer rode or attempted to influence their behavior other than to stand for the farrier to trim, or get their shots in spring and fall. Pasture ornaments.

I had some wives, one who liked horses, two who didn't. When they died of old age on my place—the horses, not the wives—I had a friend doze a hole, we rolled the old guy into it, covered it up. You were not supposed to do this, but they might as well be buried in the pasture they spent their lives in. Their spirits liked familiar pastures, I thought. The ex-wives were still whinnying, with some herd or another.

So, horses. That was why I was up on hay bales that day. I didn't know what happened—heat confusion, dehydration, whatever, but I was stacking hay on a trailer and was maybe four bales high, misstepped, fell on the trailer side, broke my left arm. I blacked out for a bit, became nauseous, sweated big. I had already hauled sixty bales to my barn and stacked it. This was the remainder, forty bales. I had maybe thirty-five on the trailer. I dragged five more on, drove home, and stacked all but thirteen one-handed, couldn't do any more, but I did get them all into the barn and shut the sliding doors. Then off to the ER.

I supposed my old man was a reason for this macho display, me always trying to live up to some movie version he had of himself. John Wayne was his hero. And the forecast called for rain that night. I didn't want to ruin my arm and the hay both.

I was hoping the arm wasn't really broken but when I tried to crank the truck wheel, backing the trailer, something wasn't working from the elbow on. No bones sticking through, though, like last time. It was the same arm I'd busted ten years before, full of metal plates and pins and screws. It set off the metal detectors in airports after that, causing waves of mistrustful consternation from the guard services. Now there's more metal in it. Boarding is a slow process for me, not that I fly much.

The arm was in a sling and a bionic-looking brace, and I experienced dull aches that made me less than effervescent. Plus I hated like hell to keep explaining the thing to everyone.

So I wasn't anxious to attend a meeting of the local

zoning board of which I'm a member. The other members were town businessmen, farmers, and various luminaries. I didn't do much. I was on the town Beautification Advisory Council. The board sought me out as representing The Arts.

I signed on, thinking I might pepper the area with strategically priced welded steel sculptures, but that hadn't happened so far. My main reason for attending, now, was a real estate lady on the board who I always liked seeing, a handsome fortyish woman with auburn hair and a great figure on the cusp of plumpness but just short of that. Good legs. Green eyes. Whitened smile that made me aware of my own beige choppers. Rita. Sometimes we had a drink in town at the faux Italian cafe on the square, once, dinner at the new motel south of town. There was electricity or something fun between us, though it could be all me and my imagination. At my advanced age, you needed a good imagination.

I had fantasized about looking at a model home with her, she locking the door after we entered, chatting about adjustable rates and balloon payments while I gazed into those green eyes.

"Wait'll you see this master bedroom, Austin."

"Lead me there, Rita."

ᜒᜒᜒ

The meeting place was always at The Golden Angus,

a good steakhouse with banquet rooms in back for wedding rehearsal dinners and meetings like ours. It was a pleasant place for a town our size. Our phone book was a slim affair with about ten yellow pages, maybe 8,000 souls spread over three counties. The town itself, Winchester, Kansas, was around 2,000. I lived maybe ten miles from it, but close enough to be on the Rural Water District.

I parked the truck behind Rita's silver Acura, half a block from the restaurant, and took my time checking my image in the window of a tattoo parlor, next to a gift shop that was having a half-off sale on crystal. I wondered how some of these businesses kept going. With my corduroy sport coat hanging over my sling I looked a little like I was affecting a cape. But my hair wasn't too wild, my jeans were clean, and I had scrubbed my welder's hands. Time to slide on into this place, get the arm stuff out of the way.

"Austin, what the hell did you do to your arm?" This from Ralph Nichols who owned the Nichols lumberyards and a big grocery store. "What's that body armor on it?"

"Improves my pitch. Wait'll softball season."

"One a those sculptures fall on you?"

His lovely white-haired wife pitched in with an "Awwww" and she patted the arm lightly, "What happened, Austin?"

This went on until we were all seated at the long table, I did a quickie one-fits-all explanation and talk turned to weather, cattle, and local news. I sat across from Rita.

She smiled, shook her head in commiseration. "Good thing you're right-handed."

This caused a little hitch in the conversation. Several thought there was more to us than there actually was.

There were about eight of us at the table, town fathers even older than I, some young Jaycees, the usual group. Ralph gaveled it to order with an empty water glass as the waitress brought us our coffee and cinnamon rolls.

"Short meeting today, ladies and gentlemen. Only one order of business. Names to consider for the new subdivision. We don't have many, so we'd like you each to come up with five or six before Halloween and submit them by phone or email to Irene here. It's an upscale area so try for elegance—"

There was a small commotion at the door to the meeting room, as Johnny Brandt bustled in calling over his shoulder. "Hell, it's noon somewhere, bring me a shot and a beer."

Johnny was the errant son of the owner of the local funeral home, on and off the wagon, occupying the off position at present. He had been on the board during one of his longer attempts at sobriety, but he rarely attended anymore.

"Cuntshire," he barked at Ralph, "That's sort of elegant. It's the shire that does it, see? British."

There was silence in the room. Johnny hated the subdivision. The present owners had bought the 300 acres from his father, Augie Brandt, and Johnny had looked upon it as his to inherit. He had talked often of a cattle operation on those acres.

"Shylock Downs." Johnny grinned angrily at Harv Rosen, the oldest insurance provider in Winchester, whose face colored instantly, as he glared back. "What do you think, Rita?" Johnnie continued. "You sold the son-ofabitch. Man, you do look good in those tight black pants. Say, I got a parcel you might like to handle—"

"Get this punk out of here." I heard my voice in a higher register than I meant it to be as I stood up.

Ralph Nichols was up at the same time, saying something like, "Johnny, that's way more than enough outa you."

The next thing I knew, Johnny was in front of me. "I guess you'll have one of your dumbass junk horses out in front of the entrance for twenty grand or so, am I right, Pops? Punk this, you fucking geezer."

Then he shoved me hard and down I went on the bad arm. I saw stars and a collection of moving legs around me as I tried to crawl out of the way.

Two of the younger men trundled him out, still flinging possible names over his shoulder, "Peckerwood Estates! Dickwick Acres! Fuckhaven Commons!" And then he was gone.

I was a little embarrassed, but couldn't fathom why,

as none of it was my fault. A drunk had called me names and pushed me over a chair in a cheap shot. With a good arm, I'd have slapped that little jaybird cross eyed.

As we sat in Rita's front seat, a soft drizzle began to mist the windshield. She took my good hand. "I really think we should go to emergency and get an X-ray of that arm, Austin."

"It's a waste of time and money, Rita, really. It's well-protected by that brace and doesn't even hurt. Believe me, if I thought there was any possibility it was injured again, I'd be there."

"Do it for me, Austin. And I'll do something really nice for you."

"I hate that place. Something really nice?"

She smiled and turned the ignition on.

&sc&s

After an hour's wait, a lead apron was tossed against my chest, a buzz, repositioning of my arm, another buzz, some more waiting.

I was reminded how much I despised emergency rooms by a strangely hyper rural family, who occupied most of the waiting room, from little kids to a bearded old man older than I.

They all seemed to be on crack, laughing, hollering, going on about nothing. The children were encouraged to race up and down the hallway by a stringy-haired woman who was relentless in her praise for their speed. The only quiet one was a large young man with either perfectly rouged red circles on his cheeks, or gin blossoms, in Carhartt coveralls on a swivel chair, testing its mechanism around to one side and back again—thunk, swivel, thunk. His eyes remained in the middle distance, trancelike.

My irritation was showing.

"It must be serious, since they brought everyone, Austin," Rita said. "No one to sit the kids I imagine. Just be patient, and we'll be on our way in no time."

What a good woman, I thought. Now that I've done this penance, I wonder what my options are, what the "something really nice" is.

"Austin Curry?" a man in a lab coat questioned the room in general.

I raised my good hand, and we followed him down a hallway, where he swiped a card and a door opened.

"And you are a relative?" he asked Rita.

"Yep, the missus," I said, just to cut through the possibility she wouldn't be allowed to go along.

She squeezed my arm against her breast and I winked at her. The doctor paused only slightly to check out this younger wife over the tops of his specs.

"Good to be careful, Miz Curry, Mr. Curry, but I think we're okay." He slapped an X-ray to a light box, showing the mass of metal in that arm. "I'm Dr. Trabon. This is the old injury," he said, pointing to the lower batch of plates and pins. "This is the new one." Whitish line up higher. "No new problems here. At least I don't see anything. Does it hurt?"

"No," I said, "I told the little woman here we didn't have to come, but you know how…" I let that trail off, and Rita pinched my good arm.

"You have pain medication?" he asked.

"Yes, thanks. Though I haven't had to use it lately."

"Where were you when this happened, Mr. Curry?"

"A zoning board meeting."

"Hmm. Lively meeting. Reminds me of this guy on *HeeHaw*, not on TV anymore, used to be. Anyway, he says to the doctor, 'Doc, I broke my arm in three places.' Doc says, 'Stay outa those places.'" He laughs, repeats, "Stay outa those places."

And we were free to go. One more appraising look at the missus over his glasses.

♥♥♥

It had stopped misting and the wind had picked up from the north. Leaves were flying around in little wind devils in the parking lot.

"Brrr. It's freezing out," Rita said, her arms folded around herself. "So where do Mr. and Mrs. Curry go now?"

I felt very much like saying, home, have a couple of toddies, maybe a joint, hit the hay. "Your car, turn on the heat, then we'll discuss it." I put my good arm around her as we shivered our way to the car.

ℰℐℰℐ

She drove us thirty some miles into Lawrence, Kansas, and a new restaurant on the outskirts of the college town. It was mid-afternoon and there was a nice mix of young people, students at KU, an older affluent bunch of locals, and maybe parents in for the weekend and a football game. The energy was pleasant and upbeat. I felt pretty foxy being in the company of a looker like Rita.

"Well, Austin. What are you up for?" Quite a twinkle in her eye.

"Steak. They don't even have to cook it! You?" I smiled, maybe doing some twinkling of my own.

She rested her chin on her interlaced hands while our server lighted a candle between us.

ℰℐℰℐ

The doorbell rang about 10 p.m. I thought I was dreaming. Then an insistent knocking at the door, a male voice calling "Rita. Ritahhhh!"

Gravel tossed against the bedroom window.

Roused from a sound sleep, I first registered the strange room, then Rita and the satin quilt, the big four-poster bed. Rita mumbled, turned over, and drew the quilt around her.

"Rita," I said, tapping her quilted shoulder.

She woke up immediately, sitting upright, beautiful

breasts bare in the moonlight. She got up and slipped on a nightgown-looking filmy thing.

"What's going on, Rita?"

"Oh, it's that damn ex-husband of mine."

"Why don't you just ignore it? Maybe he'll leave."

"Not Jack. Not when he's this way."

"Call the police?"

"Maybe. Let me handle it for now." The knocking was insistent. "I won't let him in. You stay right here. He doesn't know anyone's here. Your truck's back in town."

She left the room. Muffled voices at the door. Male voice alternately whining, then insistent, angry.

Rita said, "We'll talk when you're sober, if that ever occurs."

Then I heard, "Just a drink of water, Rita. Please, then I'll go, I really need a glass of water."

Shit, I thought, *that's how the whiny bastard gets in. She won't refuse. She'll hand it to him after unchaining the door. Don't do it, Rita, it's a child's ploy.*

She and I had just done about everything I knew how to do in bed and some that she added in that was astonishing. I just wanted to go back to sleep. Wake up and maybe try it again, have coffee, and go home. Now here was this moron at the door. I sighed, and started dressing.

Instead of letting the drunken ex in the door, she'd dialed the cops. Soon I saw red lights whirling on the dark bedroom ceiling. Was I remiss? Should I have inserted myself in this dumbass conversation? What would

I have done or said? I felt, again, somewhat embarrassed, twice in a span of fifteen hours or so, and again through no fault of my own. Then why the guilt at not "handling" this latest disruption? Why did I feel rather like I was caught in the act of cuckolding someone? I couldn't even leave unless I wanted to walk the five or so miles to town. Brother.

I peeked out the window. The ex was in the police car and a tow truck had arrived, hooking up to his SUV, a forlorn faded Jeep Cherokee. I knew the tow company driver, Randy Timmel. I computed the costs for no reason: bond, fine, release of vehicle, hours lost at work if the guy even worked, five hundred bucks, easy, just for bothering Rita. She was outside in a dressing gown and long down coat with the hood up, talking to Charlie Wainwright, the cop on duty. He was writing something on a clipboard. Old home week. I knew everybody out there except the previous husband.

I could see us all around the kitchen table having coffee and discussing the situation, Rita bustling about in her silk robe, pouring, me saying, "Well, Rita and I were sound asleep having just screwed our wheels off, no Viagra involved either, Charlie, I saw that look—" Winks all around, an elbow or two. "—and there's this racket outside—"

I jumped back from the window as Charlie seemed to look up at me. Maybe his lawman sense kicked in and he felt the eyes. Probably not. He was more of the Mayberry school of law enforcement. But this whole confluence of humanity was making me uncomfortable.

I heard vehicles leaving. Then some locking up sounds downstairs. Rita appeared in the semi-darkness.

"Austin, you're all dressed!"

"Well, if that guy got in, I didn't quite know what was expected of me. I could shoot him at my house."

"I'm so sorry."

"Wasn't your fault."

"Is the mood ruined, Austin? Oh, I hope not, we're so…you know, simpatico."

"I do know. And it's definitely not."

She allowed the silk robe to slide to the floor and advanced on fully-dressed me. This was all too good to be true, of course. As has been my wont over the long haul of years, when I ascribed wonderful qualities to a woman, she turned out to be crazy as a mouse in a shoebox. After helping me return to my unclothed state, she pulled the covers over us and rode me like the pony express. Pardon my ungentlemanliness. And ill-disguised glee.

It was in the morning's bright fresh light that I caught a glimpse of Rita's craziness. Part of her back and right shoulder were exposed and, as my eyes adjusted, I was a bit startled to see that it looked like someone had written a list, flush left to her spine on the right side with a black sharpie or some kind of marker. It started about four inches down from her neck and continued on under the quilt. It was a tattoo.

The letters were quite neat and looked almost printed. It was a list of names. I moved closer so I could read. She spooned into me and made a pleasure noise as I got closer, then reached around and began guiding me. I was surely aroused but also wanted to read this list. I grazed her neck with my lips and got the first name: it was Alec Thomas. The next was Joe Ramirez. Then Nick Nolte. *The actor?* What *was* this list? She pulled the quilt up. I'd have to resume my reading another time. She damn near made me forget about it.

ഇൽ

Then we did have coffee in her bright kitchen, the morning sun slanting in, catching a few dust particles.

"Rita, I haven't been bored since Johnny Brandt knocked me over that chair. I thank you, I surely do." I felt this lacked the proper complimentary tone but I'd think of something better before I left. I sipped my coffee.

"That's lovely, Austin. You have such a way about you. How do you like your eggs?"

"Any old way." I thought, *like I like my women*, but kept that one inside. And it wasn't true, anyway.

I noted she looked quite good without makeup, hair tied back with unplanned wisps here and there. The list was somewhat visible through the silk robe but only as a series of lines. I couldn't tell how far down they went. When she poured more coffee I could see a whole breast and it made me giddy and smug at the same time. She was a handsome lady all right.

"Rita, I must ask you about something," I said, before I could quite cap the well on my curiosity.

"Yes, Austin?" She was standing to my right, close enough that I could smell a faint perfume from her robe.

I chickened out. "What do you think of the age difference between you and me?"

She put the coffee pot on the table, moved behind me, put her hands on my shoulders, and began massaging my neck.

"What a question, Austin. Age. It's a number. Let's not worry about things like that, okay?" She patted my cheek, sat down across from me. "How's your arm feel?" Again, the chin on interlaced fingers, echoing her look from the restaurant in Lawrence.

"Almost as good as the rest of me. I had totally forgotten about it."

She laughed. "I'm so glad I could do that."

✦✦✦

I had her drop me off a couple of blocks from my truck, at the feed store and I pretended to head in there as she drove off. Then I walked to my truck. I think this was to save her any embarrassment from being seen dropping me off at my truck with its frosted-over windows, obviously there all night. Or maybe it was for me. I unlocked it, slid in, and started it, turned the defroster up high.

Then I glanced over at the tattoo place next to the gift store I'd seen the day before. Winchester Tattoo the sign said. I let the truck idle and walked over to the storefront, looked in the window. Sign said OPEN, one of those Walmart neon-looking things. I entered, and a tinkling sound came from a device that announced an entry.

The shop was crammed with art books and photos of tattoos, many of them prints of what looked to be local customers, bikers and musicians, some were of bare body portions, genitalia with tattoos that cleverly incorporated the parts shown, legs with zippers and floral patterns, vines, backs covered with gruesomely colored scenes, price codes, skulls, marijuana leaves, the usual, all fairly nicely drawn, if off-putting to me. I never understood the application of some non-erasable thing to the skin, like those designs young women liked to have above their butt. Then I saw it, the list. A voice behind me startled me a bit.

"Wanting a tat?"

I turned to face a rotund man in an Ed Hardy T-shirt, the art on which looked like a huge tattoo. He had a beard like ZZ Top. "Well, no, not me. Just had some questions if you don't mind."

"You a cop or somethin'?"

I chuckled. "No, no, just interested. My granddaughter just came back from California with a tattoo and I was wondering if it was safe."

"Depends. If it was done right with sterile needles, sure, it's safe. Most are. A bad experience, just one, can put you out of business so we're pretty careful."

"Did you do this list here?" I pointed to Rita's back, noting the list was maybe 30 names.

"Yeah. She's gonna run out of back on that side. Then we start on the other side. She's a good steady customer."

I looked closer at the photo. I saw Ralph Nichols on there. My dentist was listed. I felt suddenly dizzy. When that passed, I asked, "What's the story behind this list?"

"Guess I can tell you. She's pretty open about it. Brags about it even. She calls it her back list. Anyone who's had her on her back, she puts—on her back. I wouldn't mind being on the list, actually. She's hot. But I'm strictly professional. Doesn't pay to get involved with customers."

"Who's the last name on the list?"

"I dunno. She's coming in tomorrow, though. Some lucky new gent."

"Nice lettering."

"Thanks. My name's Jake, by the way." He held his hand out.

"Johnson. Jim Johnson," I said, shaking his hand.

⋅⋅⋅

They said, after the fire, that arson was suspected.

Rita's smoke detector didn't work and she perished in the blaze. That's how the county gazette put it—perished. I wish, now, I had read the entire list because that would probably include the person or persons who had done the thing, if, indeed someone had done it, but I only remembered a couple of names. And who would be compromised by it, anyway?

I had been going to distance myself from Rita, but only because she was a little scary in my book, not because I'd be on her list. Curiously, I didn't mind that at all. When I thought to drop by and ask Jake where the list photo was, he said "What list?"

The new red Dodge king-cab dually sitting in front of his shop told me that perhaps he'd been bought off, and that, in turn, narrowed the list to a few wealthy businessmen. But I hadn't seen the whole list, so that really told me nothing.

Her ex-husband was held for a while but they finally turned him loose.

The first name on the list, I saw in the obituary, was an uncle, her mother's brother. And that, to me, was a sad deal. I attended a couple more board meetings but it was terrible to be there, just awful.

And I caught Ralph Nichols staring at me at the last one, with a hard look. *He's running for state senate unopposed. And, come to think of it, Irene is the one with the money.*

I just bought some new smoke detectors and a yappy

little Jack Russell Terrier that barks at anyone approaching the house, me included. And I had a .357 with one birdshot shell in the cylinder for the first shot, .38 specials for the rest.

My arm was okay, less range of motion than I'd like, and weather changes affected it. The slight pain reminded me of Rita, and my dentist. I wondered, should I change dentists? Nick Nolte remained a mystery, though there's an N. Nolte listed in our little phone book.

COFFIN A CARLOAD

I grew up in a lot of places. Revise that. I lived in a lot of places. Some of them odd. Once, we lived in New York, Manhattan Island, just on the cusp of Harlem, One-Hundred-Twentieth Street, almost Canada, where my stepfather hailed from. I was maybe six. I was bundled up, sent out to the city bus with a note on my Michelin-like snowsuit, to attend some kind of pre-school—this would be grounds for a child services abuse summons these days. I once fell asleep on the bus and rode to the end of the line and the folks had to send a cab to come get me. That was a needless expense at a time when we couldn't afford such shenanigans. I was, myself, a needless expense, actually.

Somehow, I was shunted down south with my abso-lutely needless expense of a half-sister—six years older than me and exhibiting many of the characteristics of a serial killer, but she didn't blossom that way, luckily enough for the world around her—who had a different father than I did. We had the mother in common.

We were left with our step-grandparents. Pop, my step-grandfather was an Episcopal minister, born in London. He talked funny and was a strict disciplinarian. So we went to church regularly. I had to keep my locutionary guard up so I didn't blurt a Pop-ism like say something was "too dear" instead of too expensive. Stuff like that got you beat up in town. Pop didn't have to worry. He had the armies of God on his side, but I was fair game. All these step and half people were results of my mom's three marriages: first was a guy before my time who owned radio stations and that's all I know about him. He never showed up again. Then, my dad, a track star—approached Jesse Owens's time in the 100—a snappy dresser and a great dancer. Then the Atomic Bomb Guy, Pop's son—more later about him. Divorces were looked upon as character flaws or promiscuity, or worse, back then and maybe they were. Mine could be attributed to all that and more. Maybe it was just a form of Attention-Deficit Hyperactivity Disorder.

Anyway, this was in Louisiana, near swamps that I recall fairly vividly. A little town where I saw chain gangs working on the roads. And they weren't singing folk songs.

Once when I asked my stepfather why Pop and Mother-B chose to live down there, I was given one of my first object lessons about toadying to The Man.

Pop had originally had a church in a wealthy area in the South, a cigarette-manufacturing town, and a well-dressed member of the congregation had paused to talk to him after the service. This person offered him a cigarette from what had to be a pack of Lucky Strikes—although I'd have preferred it had been a pack of Camels and I don't mind telling you why in another digression further along.

The man had said, "Have one. Not a cough in a carload."

Pop declined, being a non-smoker even then, in the 1940s, saying, "Perhaps not, but every one is a nail in your coffin," no doubt pleased with the morphological riposte.

The well-dressed church member turned out to be a VIP with American Tobacco Company and Pop was transferred to the Episcopal equivalent of Lower Slobbo-via. He carried on as usual, said what he pleased, and, who knows, saved a soul or two.

I was young when I heard this story, seven or therea-bouts, but knew it contained a seed of warning not to smart off at well-dressed, influential people. I had heard the story in a sort of aural dyslexia, however, as concern-ing coffins in carloads and nails in them, but still got the import. Always take a cigarette when offered, especially Luckies, and just say "Thank you," and shut up. Smart off and they'll move you to the swamps.

The swamps. Bayous. Bored to the maximum, as only a seven-year-old can be, I ventured into an Amazonian area that was probably off limits one sunny day. I say probably, because, come to think of it, no one had ever said to me, "Do Not Go Into The Swamps," or, "Do Not Play In Heavy Traffic, while in NY." In fact, such activity might well have been encouraged.

I chose to explore. It grew darker as I explored farther. The ground was marshy and tales of quicksand came to mind as I thrilled myself with danger.

Fallen trees and vines obstructed my path, and then I found myself in a cavernous place that was open enough but not to the sky, being covered above by overgrowth. It was, of course dim in this place, cypress trees stretching their visible roots into surrounding water. I looked around for 'gators. None visible, but they were known to appear like logs and, snap! That was the end of you.

"We always told him not to go into the swamp."

"No you didn't!"

My sister told me to forget 'gators. She said that alligator-gar fish would get me even in my bed. That they walked by night right up to the house to get pecans from the tree in front. That the bayou was full of them.

It smelled nose-wrinkling awful in there. Swamp gas, dead growth, stagnant water. My eyes adapted to the darker surroundings. Oh my God, what was *that?* A big dead thing, legs in the air, vultures stalking around it like evil little men in overcoats!

I ran, I fell, I got up, ran some more, fell some more,

hollering, gasping, I think even praying. Sunlight, blessed safety! Breathing in shrieks like a distance runner fallen on the cinder track, I willed myself to the screen door, inside. When I could breathe more normally, I pulled a Royal Crown Cola out of the icebox, poured it with shaky hands into a thick glass tumbler—whatever happened to those squat, barrel-shaped glasses anyway? I'd like to have a set. Used to be they were in rural cafes everywhere. The kind with screen doors that had bread advertisements on them.

Down there Royal Crown was pronounced Arruh See. I drank my Arruh See, cold fizz burning my throat, life returning to my limbs. The dead thing was bovine in nature, I later figured out. Years later. Then, however, it was a swamp monster, a bigfoot, before I'd ever heard of such a thing. If a swamp monster could come to such an end in the bayou, why would I ever venture near one again? The Atomic Bomb Guy, that's why.

He took me duck hunting in the bayou. Since I was stupid—it's pronounced sty-u-pid, not stoo-pid, styupid —he figured, I could at least be macho. I was armed with a sixteen-gauge pump shotgun which I hated to fire because it made my shoulder black and blue, but I learned not to mention it. And Susie, a sweet old water spaniel was with us, as we rowed between cypress trees to an open spot that looked promising. Ducks did fly over but too high. To Atomic's ever-lasting chagrin, I led a duck by fifteen feet, fired, and down it fell. The only duck of the day. Susie leaped into the water and swam through cypress roots to get it, brought it to us, and we helped her back into the boat before alligators ate her up. It was a lucky shot, or, to me, unlucky. I hated having killed this beautifully colored bird. And I would be further resented. It was sort of like beating your martial arts instructor, something I did, later in life when I'd had enough. From then on it was a hard go in that class. Going up against The Man has a price.

ℰ✶ℰ✶

I took my RC to the bench beneath the pecan tree. Clouds scudded overhead and I thought hard about my real father, tried to conjure his face among the clouds, wished for those times with him when no wars worried, the house in Kansas City, darkening on steamy days like this, heavy velvet curtains separating rooms, deadening sound, conserving cool, oscillating fans humming, their summer buzz as comforting as their breeze, that house where my grandmother and father and aunt all lived, finally renting rooms to keep that house we loved. My summers there were filled with the opposite of worry. The tension melted, the only scares being delicious ones when my dad would pop up from the heavily curtained dining room moo-haha and chase me screaming through the house, catch me, tickle me until I screeched with that unmistakably real-kid laughter and lightly peed my pants.

Tall stacked cloudscud in fanciful figures, floaters to a boy's summer-stormed eye. Pirate hat and horse's head disintegrated and molded a dog, a camel, a passing buxom babe, busted by wind, became a fearsome face. Fat chance drops of rain forced my focus on the stuccoed house, and home sweet home formed a safe shield from lightning where heavy velvet curtains divided darkened rooms and his father foxtrotted alone to Cole Porter arms encircling an incorporeal partner, and thunder mumbled as distance pulled it taut as an engine with boxcars bumping groaning yet loosening as it faded to naught.

ꜱꜱꜱ

In Louisiana, I witnessed, every Sunday, the beheading of a luckless chicken on a stump in the backyard. It was allowed to run around until it expired. I watched this in silence with slit eyes that went from the choppee to the choppor, Mother B. my stepgrandmother, a cool customer when it came to killing. This facet of her didn't escape my notice. At any rate, I never connected that bizarre event with what appeared on the table later that day. After church and the voodoo chicken ritual, I was left to my devices.

I was often alone in this rural place. Wandering. I must have done that a lot. This particular wanderlust brought me to yet another bovine event that terrified me more than the bayou incident.

Gravel road, kicking stones as I walked, going no-where in particular. It was hot. Clouds curled and un-curled in the afternoon sky, stacked and fell, became ob-jects, and floated away. I stopped. Something was behind me, maybe a city block back. If it was The Bully, I would have to haul ass and evade, a survival technique I'm sure Navy SEALs have in their repertoire. He asked me why I said comics instead of funny books. "What are those pants you wear that make noises? Corduroys?"

A holdover from New York winters.

"Never heard of such a dumb thing. You a Yankee?"

But it wasn't Bubba or Junior or whatever they called him. It was a bull! It was galloping! Shitfire and save matches as Junior was wont to say. I turned and hauled ass, the fire-breathing thing gaining on me. I had seen charging bulls in comics, in movies. They showed no mercy. Steam came out of their nostrils. Why such an animal was allowed to exist I had no clue, but I knew they did, like the hornet, like the mean dog, like swamp creatures.

I ran. At first I yelled along with the running. But that wasn't propelling me any faster, even *I* knew that. Fence posts were my measure of speed. They flashed by. But how long could I keep up this dervish speed in a straight line? And was I faster than a bull? No, it turned out, the thing was gaining. Now something was coming the other way, good God, another bull? No, a flivver car/pickup vehicle. I ran in front of it and it stopped.

An ancient black man was driving. "Somp'n scairt you, boy?" He was dressed in overalls, an engineer's cap on his head. He looked warily around. "Kin I carry you somwhere's?"

I thought, *Well, why would you do that if you can give me a ride? But, sure, yes, if you have to, I'm desperate.*

"Uh, could I get a ride just down the road?" I pointed to where the bull had been. There was no bull. I blinked.

He indicated the doorless passenger side, and I was in like a shot. He dropped me off in my front yard, and I thanked him profusely. He dismissed it with a small motion of his hand as though waving away a fly.

He chuckled. "I know your grampa, boy. I'll get me a ticket to heaven."

What happened to the bull? *Was* it a bull? Now, I think it was most probably a steer or heifer, out of a pasture. When it saw me, it was curious. When I ran, it loped along behind. But it must have turned off somewhere. I remember it as one of the scariest events in my young life. I shared it with no one to this day. Now that I read it, it seems banal and dopey. Well, what are young lives for if not to spice up stuff for their inhabitants? Reaching back into that day, I do see a bull. How he disappeared, I've no clue.

Could this be why my event in rodeo was bullriding? Not consciously. And I wasn't very good at it, but I faced my fears and paid my fees and finally, in Santa Maria, rode to the buzzer and caught a compliment from world champion Gary Leffew. But the ligaments were ripped from my right arm, and I retired winless with no big buckle to flash my accomplishments, just one that I got by placing in a jackpot rodeo in Kansas. Bullriding was, as I looked back now, inexplicable. Who needed to buy danger when it lurked for free?

Gradually I learned the cadences and vernacular of down South and began to modify my Yankee-ness, even with Pop around to lead me astray. I knew not to trust his oddball language, even though his smallish congregation seemed to delight in it. But I also learned that Cajun wasn't the way to go. I loved what I heard of it but I couldn't butcher a sentence in that wonderful special way. I couldn't really say to Mother B., for example, "C'mere minute ago sumbitch gimme dat orange, *nest' ce pas?*"

In town there was one movie house, named Bruno's. If you went to the feature and paid the dime or whatever it was back then, you could go see it again and again for free until the next one. Then on Saturdays, there were serials and you were expected to get new tickets for those. I remember all this imperfectly I'm sure but who's going to tell me I'm wrong? Bruno? Not likely. "He doin' de long Fais-do-do," as Bruno himself might say. The Fais-do-do being the go-to-sleep dance. The long dirt nap to some.

Emmylu, the evil sister, oddly enough, I don't re-member as even being around, except in those instances where she would suddenly appear and offer me a thousand dollars if I would apply the palm of my hand to an iron she swore was cold, or some similar devious plan. Perhaps Mother B. had her boiling clothes, or something I was too young or useless for. Skinning hogs. Churning butter. More likely she was reading *True Confessions* and movie magazines in the sunroom where Pop raised orchids.

They moved Pop to Winchester, Kentucky. Maybe he pissed off a dignitary, maybe it was a promotion. All I know is it was a bigger house, there were two Irish Setters, Champagne and Red, and an uncle, Doug, lived there, took me into the hills to shoot his .22 and he let me play with his old electric train. That, and my real father appearing at the end of the war. He was in a sailor suit, white hat cocked on his head, carrying a duffel. In my memory, I saw him at the end of a long, long, tree-tunneled street and ran to him as fast as I ran from that bull.

The reason my stepfather and mother were never around during these years was my stepfather was involved in the Manhattan Project. He spent a lot of time in Los Alamos, and Oak Ridge, Tennessee, working on a component of the atomic bomb—a switch, he later told me, and that was all he would tell me. But he had books about nuclear fission in his library. He was an electrical engineer who had gone to college early when most kids his age were sophomores in high school. He was not a bundle of fun. I found a plaque in the basement from the AEC that thanked him and twenty-two others for their part in the Japanese surrender in WWII. There was a list of twenty-three men, one of which was him. He used to get drunk each year at the anniversary of the atomic bomb blast, August, around the time of my birthday.

My mom—now there was a fascinating person. I can see her now, at a house party, rugs rolled back for dancing, lots of drinking going on. She had a martini in one hand, a cigarette in the other, and she was dancing alone to "Rum and Coca Cola," a song about the "Yankee dollah," or a Tex Beneke record. If she didn't like a record, she would drop it on the tile floor and shatter it. She hated "Pistol Packin' Mama." Crash!

I would be given orange juice glasses of beer at these affairs. Practicing to be a lush at eight years old. Turned out I was a natural. Had to call it quits on that finally. She never quit, however. Died of lung cancer, smoked up to the very end. Anyway, you know that movie, *She's Out Of Your League*? Well, the Atomic Bomb Guy was the geek, she was the hot girl. I never saw her that way as a kid—your mother is just your mother. Saw it later in photos. Thing is, the Atomic Bomb Guy, Ed, wasn't as nice as the geek in the movie. He talked of niggers, Jews, fairies, micks, dagos. Seems he had it in for a lot of folks. It was a wonder I wasn't a stone racist. But he was devoted to my mom. Subservient even. And he remained that way to her death. They took lots of trips when my sister and I were kids, didn't take us along. They knew how to have a good time. And we were dumped off at respective grandparents for summers. They had it made. Had fun, too, from what I gathered—Vegas, Curacao, Montana, Europe. They finally settled on Maui and spent months every year there, had a circle of friends on the island.

She once drove a Packard to Chicago from Kansas City, her birthplace and our home off and on over the years. It ran out of oil and she drove it until it stopped. All they had to do was pour more oil in it and off she drove again. Another object lesson for me: buy Packards.

She was given an Auburn Boattail convertible as a teen. Her own parents were well-to-do, if not wealthy. Her father was a lawyer and DA, appointed by Harding. Once when he was reading the paper, I remarked that he looked like Harry Truman. I had a facility for voicing such unsolicited observations, sort of like Pop. He snapped the paper, said to my grandmother, "Byrd, can you find this boy something to do?"

Those grandparents liked my real old man. They thought the Atomic Bomb Guy was a smartass. My favorite grandparents were my real dad's parents—kind, like he was. A bit preoccupied but kindness more than made up for the sometimes distant, off in another world-ness, I sometimes encountered. They were fond of music, dancing, sherry, each other, and me.

The bomb guy used to tell me I was stupid, even though I had blown the tops off two Stanford Binet tests, which I wasn't supposed to know. I think he thought I couldn't be very smart, not being a blood relative to him. He wasn't physically abusive, I'm thankful for that. But he sneered a lot. I got used to it. I don't use his name here, but I actually did respect the man at certain times in my life. He was honest enough, he worked hard, he took me hunting and to the oil patch in Tulsa sometimes to accompany him on fieldwork. I noticed, when he was with other men in the field, he would get all western—this was in Tulsa—and call me "boy" when he'd tell me to do something. He would tell them a joke and when it came to the punch line he would put a hand on someone's shoulder and look down at his shoes—cowboy boots while in Tulsa, odd for a Canadian who, to my knowledge, had never been near a horse. But he did like John Wayne. Anyway, he'd pause and act like he was hiccupping or something, shaking his head in apparent wonder, hardly contained, and out it would come—the punch line. He was not only an engineer, he was a salesman, it turned out, for whatever company he was with. He must have been good at it, as he died a millionaire, back when that meant something. He built his own office building which he sold to a Japanese group for another mil or so. Some irony there.

Back to Camel Cigarettes. Tom Robbins really did a number on them some years ago with *Still Life with Woodpecker*, a thoroughly enjoyable novel that was billed, I think, as a love story that happens inside a pack of Camels. At one point in this wonderful book, I was instructed to hold a Camels pack up to a mirror, but I can't remember what I was supposed to see. Something "palindromatic," I think, but I didn't see it. I remember thinking LEMAC doesn't read the same forward and backward, but *something* was supposed to.

I wasted five or six minutes of my young life on it. Nothing but mosques on the back.

Reminds me of when a girl/woman in my young life brightly inquired, "Wanna do it upside down and backward?"

I said, "Sure!" but, to this day have no idea what she was talking about.

It never came up again, so I assumed we did it. Or forgot it.

Back to Camels. I didn't start smoking until I was in college. I don't recall buying the Camels but I must have gotten them at the Phillips 66 where I worked after classes. I do remember the hit. The soft explosion in my brain. I was walking from campus to the fraternity house annex and I lit a Camel. Inhaled it, at first, shallowly. Then more boldly. The autumn colors around me became intensified, saturated. A sense of well-being settled on me. In those few seconds I became a smoker. I could probably find that street, that exact spot, if I cared to. I was hooked.

Some useless fat ass at R.J. Reynolds, like that nettlesome dude who banished my step-grandfather, was getting richer as I headed hell bent toward emphysema and a rich assortment of diseases.

I'd walk a mile for a Camel. Not a cough in a carload. Nine out of ten doctors. Give 'em a carton for Christmas. One ad said "More doctors smoke Camels than any other brand!" And wasn't there a photo of a doctor in a white smock, graying temples, holding a smoking Camel in his hand? Yes!

The Mad Men plotted with the nicotine dealers and we all smoked. I went into advertising—never worked on a tobacco account but I'd have plotted right along with them. I did work on booze and beer long before MADD, long before "responsible drinking." Smoked, drank, and drove with the worst of them. DUIs were regarded as a minor offense. A beloved aunt died of emphysema, and my mother died the same week of lung cancer. I smoked in the hallways of their hospitals as I paced. As they slipped away. It would be another ten years before I quit smoking.

But Camels. I see the older package, and it fills me with nostalgia. It becomes benign. The mosques, the pyramids, the dromedary, and the Rick's Place, Casablanca, feeling of it all. The Tom Robbins effect. It's all tied up with my youth, my own lost generation, the promises and marriages and the messes we left behind. Palm trees! I love palm trees. When things got bad, I went where the palm trees were. Florida, LA, Hawaii, the Bahamas. And things did get better inside the Camel package. I imagined things and they happened. In Los Angeles I imagined Raymond Chandler and hand-tinted postcards and mysterious assignations and Toyota commercials, and they all happened. Paunchy producers in cashmere sweaters said "Trust Me." They said, "The screenplay will write itself."

In Westwood, I bought three-foot horus figures at an Egyptologist's, figures that had been in DeMille's Cleopatra. I may have been "Someone Else." There were Asian girls and mercenaries. Palm trees. My black Cadillac Touring Coupe would glide through Beverly Hills. Perhaps I looked like a gynecologist on the way up. I was trying for Conway Twitty.

When I climbed out of the LA Camel pack, I traded for a GMC truck with dual rear wheels and scrammed back to Kansas. I lit up the highways. I don't know who I was on the way back, but I only stopped for gas and Denny's Grand Slams. Oh, and to look up a trick rider with a little broken nose in Dalhart, Texas, who had once been the center of my world many years before. She was not there.

But after I paid at Denny's, the attractive cashier lady smiled and said, "There. Now we're on speaking terms again." The trick rider would have said such a thing. A non sequitur but charming. I fled to my truck before I fell in love.

❧❧❧

I smoked and drove, drove and smoked. I crushed Camel packs and tossed them in the bed, in the extended cab area, under the dashboard. They piled up and reflected the fractured light that crushed magic containers do, the lights of tractor trailers and trains that I raced alongside, and lights of towns whose signs proclaimed *Resume Speed*. There were several with that name. When you're driving at night through deserts, you see things. A huge bird swooped at me, causing me to duck. Light balls played along the road, matching my speed. A camel crossed the road at the edge of my bright headlights and lumbered into the darkness. It wasn't a deer as deer are notoriously suicidal, waiting for the exact moment to leap into your lights. Camels are into self-preservation. They carry extra water and spit at humans. They aren't fools.

I pulled in for gas at another town named Resume Speed, broke my pattern of Denny's Grand Slams for something that was similar at a ramshackle café, sat next to Death Valley Scottie or someone very like him at the counter. Beat up old hat, brim pushed up in front. Emulating that cartoon? He looked at me. Hopefully, the Los Angeles was fading. My hair was wild I saw in a reflection in the round pie display.

"Howdy," I said, nodding. The first word I'd said to a human for a while, other than, "Grand Slam, please." It sounded odd to me, croaking.

He concentrated on his eggs after grunting something.

"I saw a camel," I said. He grunted again.

"Last night. Maybe I dreamed it up."

"There's camels out there," he said. "World War Two, they used 'em for desert training. They bred. Wild. Don't see 'em much." Back to his eggs.

I realized who he looked like. That cartoon character they put on mud flaps with the words "Back Off." Can't think of his name. Yosemite Sam!

He finished his eggs, slurped the dregs of his coffee, wiped his cartoon mouth with the paper napkin, and turned on his stool toward me. He looked at me with an unnerving intensity and began speaking, "The Northern Lights have seen queer sights—"

"I heard *that,* " I said.

He shushed me then proceeded to give me the whole rendition of "The Cremation of Sam McGee" in an unblinking, almost angry recitation. When he finished, he said to the counterman/cook, "He's got it," indicating me with a thumb, walked out.

His entire tab was $80 and change, but I refused and paid only his breakfast, $3.50. With my breakfast, two packs of Camels, free Zippo, and tip, I was out of there for less than ten dollars. Plus, I had three chances on an old "Saharan Sands" punchboard game. It had a Fatima-like dancing girl on it in transparent veils...and, yes, a camel, some pyramids, and palm trees. I won on all three rolled-up papers I pushed through the little holes. I won a Zippo, and the two packs of Camels. The counterman/owner was becoming rankled so I quit.

An overweight but pretty girl in overalls, creamy bare shoulders, and earmuffs entered The Resume Speed Café and sat in a booth. She said "I'd walk a mile for a Camel," to no one in particular, it seemed. I shook one up for her on my way out. She took it and said, "I'd do any fucking thing for a carton. Get my drift?"

I exited hurriedly. I'd wanted to ask about the earmuffs but decided it would be best left one of those mysteries. Earmuffs at ninety in the shade. I still wonder.

The big dually was a gas hog but I had plans for it once in Kansas and settled. I would once again have horses, and I would haul them places in a long stock trailer. Unlike the cowboy-boot-wearing atomic bomber, I wore mine with pride and authenticity. Though, I had as often found myself horseback with PF Flyers and a baseball cap. Horses attracted women. I had learned that over the years and through a couple of marriages. The women they attracted were not always beneficial to conventions such as marriage. Nor were they women especially good for centering one's inner core. Often they were young and indiscriminate. As an ex-wife would say, "He thought those damn dirty-leg women wanted to buy his horses. Nobody wanted to buy his horses."

Aahh, but the camel that broke the straw: I saw the signs. They'd been there all along. I passed a truck that had a picture of a running camel on the trailer, and it said "Humpin' to Please." I believe the name of the outfit was Campbell 66 Express. But, by then, camels were everywhere. On barn sides, on grocery store walls, a tin sign making up the floor of a rat hot rod I walked by in a Denny's parking lot. So, was it a surprise, when in Resume Speed, Texas, that I was handed a flyer for a charity carnival and raffle and one of the grand prizes was a camel and trailer? Was I surprised when I was born? I don't know, but it probably seemed equal parts natural and WTF crazy. The auction was the following day. I cruised around, found a nice motel, The Royal Crown, with a Jacuzzi and bubble bath. It even had a restaurant and a bar/nightclub. I was ready for such a thing. Ready teddy. And a prime rib.

I emerged from my room, smelling like an Esquire magazine full of aftershave sniffers. I wore fresh Wranglers, spit-polished ostrich-skin boots, a 1938 Mickey-Mouse-scowling-and-looking-mean T-shirt, and a pinstripe Brooks Brothers natural shoulder blazer. I was loaded for camel. This was only the warmup though, the night before the Big Game.

The restaurant was full of truckers, townies dressed up and down, families driving through. I got a Manhattan and a Prime Rib, medium-rare, house salad with ranch, and I dove in. Hot cornbread and real butter. I had a booth and the house was full. The night was right. If there'd been a casino, I would have taken it down. I pulled the flyer out of my breast pocket when I'd ordered coffee and took in the headline: Camels and Cars and Carnival Time! Car Show and Carnival to benefit Children's Hospital! The date was the next day.

There were pictures of classic cars, carnival rides, Shriners, and a photo of a camel with a trailer. The blurb beneath it read: Win this trained circus camel and trailer, or $1000 cash! Raffle tickets available now—$5 each!

At each corner of the flyer were pyramids, palm trees, and the Camel cigarette pack dromedary. Something told me one ticket would get me this camel, whether I wanted it or not. I lit a Camel, paid my ticket, left a tip. The bar beckoned with music and hubbub. A neon sign said RC's Oasis. I remember thinking the old RC bottle had palm trees and pyramids on it. Like the Camels package.

The bar featured a singing group called The Camelettes, a trio of fine-looking middle aged, or older, women. All blondes, one had heavy metal goldilocks, one had a chic short cut that hung down in her face on one side, and one was practically crewcut. Hot women. The minimal stage setting was, yes, pyramids, palm trees, a camel. It looked like a pack of cigarettes. They were all dressed in matching colors, beige to camel, sequined, tight-fitting short cocktail dresses. Bass player, lead singer with microphone, one played cocktail drums. They all sang. As I walked in, the song was *Canadian Sunset*. Their harmony was intoxicating and so were the drinks. I was their biggest fan. They were beautiful. I could see they were older, but they just had softer edges and their blonde hair was backlit by the display. They sang "I Remember You," and "Blue Moon," and "Sentimental Journey" and classics that evoked my childhood beer drinking days, when promise floated about like the cigarette smoke and the laughter of the adults. I sent them requests: "Small Hotel," "One More For The Road," "Midnight Sun," "Summer Wind." They knew them all. They were magic, and I was drunk. The last thing I remember with any clarity was telling them I loved them and would be honored to have them with me the rest of my life. Sex only if they wanted it, and I surely hoped they would be amenable to it. Their children were older than me one said and kissed me chastely.

"Think nothing of it," I said inhaling her perfume that was probably sold in a green crystalline art deco bottle in a bazaar on the silk road in 1922 to a gentleman in a wrinkled linen suit and pith helmet for three cartons of Camels and a small suede bag of gold Kroners.

I dreamed, or maybe we *were* at the motel pool, some pool, that night, the moon was high, and there was a shower of sequins as dresses were unzipped and tossed on a chaise in a pile of cold-flash starlit diamonds. Around the pool were no idling Kenworths or silent SUVs in the shadows, no vehicles at all it seemed. If anything, the surrounding landscape was moon-swept smooth dunes melting into a Maxfield Parrish sky but my attention was on the shimmery figures in the moonlit pool, and all the lights were off except, perhaps, some blue ones underwater. These beautiful blue-skinned women of the MILF variety swam and played, turned and slid and sped, one popping up by where I lay transfixed, beckoned me in, her hair sleeked back. I stripped to briefs and dove in. I was tossed and turned as if by porpoises, played with, teased, released, rolled over and over, handled by many hands, kissed on the lips underwater and given air, CPR of the soul and I could feel her smile, her tongue, my hands slipped and slid on water slick breasts, a rib cage, then she was gone in a quick kick, and I floated to the top, gulped air, pulled down again by two pairs of hands. The blueminescence and the buoyancy were exhilarating, and they dragged me to a shallow end where we performed acts of affection, standing, sitting, splashing. I was weightless. I saw stars, and I heard them sing, or maybe it was the sisters, slowly, melodiously in a register only whales would hear, "The Campbells are coming, Hooray, Hooray..." and I said, "Me too," and was carried to piles of Bedouin tasseled cushions in the night oasis breeze and slept, the bubbling spring that fed the pool the only sound.

ϾϿϾϿ

I woke up feeling pretty good for having poured in so many after-dinner drinks at the motel lounge the night before. I had a vague memory of swimming, then the dream came back full-force. I wanted to retain it, a keep-sake. I had never had such a lovely dream, one that didn't turn on me and become nightmarish with free falls and being out in public in only my underwear. I stretched out in the surprisingly comfortable motel bed and reviewed what I could remember of the night and the dream that merged with it, sequencing it, savoring it. Merrilee, Louise, and Nancy, sisters, in their sixties by my deductions, all of them, and verging on voluptuous, yet petite. All around five foot. Beautiful curvy little things, one blue-eyed, the others hazel or green. And their voices, together or single, hauntingly clear and pretty. I had gotten to know them fairly well and we had chemistry, sure enough.

I colored a bit remembering how I had been their cheerleader and had gone from table to table gathering requests of the old songs, the classics. I'd danced with one and then another of them during their act, coaxing them from the raised platform, gently, pulling them close, feeling their warmth and form through the icy sequins, smelling their hair, their mysterious perfumes, twirling them by their fingertips as if choreographed. For this once, I was Astaire to their Rogers.

I'm not a dancer like my old man was, but somehow I felt like I had skimmed on air. Probably I was seen as a drunken young clown but the applause seemed genuine, enthusiastic.

Then it all sort of merged with the dream. Last call. The bartender blinking the lights and people leaving. Sitting at the darkened empty bar with the sisters and listening to them recount old gigs, dreams of stardom, the

Johnny Carson Show as children, NPR, jazz legends they knew, like Stan Kenton and Count Basie.

"Remember," said Merrilee to the others, "how Jimmy Dorsey tried to get us in bed for a four-way?" They laughed, and Nancy looked at me and said, "We're shocking you, I bet."

"A little."

"Are we disgusting? Old ladies?"

"You're beautiful. If I were Jimmy Dorsey, I'd have tried harder. Then or now."

"Right *answer*," said Merrilee, who sat closest to me. "Louise, get us all a Cointreau Double-X Special," and she squeezed my upper thigh. Louise raised her eyebrows, then smiled, and moved behind the bar. I'd swear she got something out of her purse. A small faceted vial.

❦❦❦

I believe I'll step in here. I, being whatever I feel like being, whenever I feel like being it. I was a light ball on his desert drive, for instance. I passed him in Hank Williams's Cadillac convertible and he didn't even notice. The Campbell sisters were with me, but they were along as half naked floozies of Hank's. That caper was wasted on him in his Denny's-to-Denny's red-eye odyssey. We were a bit ghostly, I suppose, could have dialed it up a bit, but didn't want him to run off the road. He was barreling and sleepy, so I aimed my big night owl at him then put a camel in front of him, lumbering across the road. Did "Sam McGee" for him at the diner. God, I love that poem. Olivier couldn't do it better. You should hear me do "The Men Who Don't Fit In." That was his old man's favorite.

Let's call him Cy. Like sigh. Or Jake. Since he's not seen fit to name himself in this whole episode. Notice that? Well, Jake is jake with me.

Moving along. Jake woke up in this Royal Crown Motel in a king sized bed, stretched and squirmed deeper into the quilts and covers, trying to remember his "dream." Louise had slipped him a sort of mickey. From my workshop. Then we took him swimming in the desert at a favorite water hole of mine. I kept the Arabs away from him. That wouldn't have been fair, like I care, but the girls had taken a shine to him. There was penetration, to all our delight. He'd have boned a camel if we'd have let him after his Cointreau Double-X Special. So, man of the hour, swimming and dabbling and the girls, playing bobbing-for-Jake and had he only seen, I made them into manatees. Ever seen a manatee? Jeezo capeezo, ugly as homegrown sin. Well, there he was, getting it on with manatees, but all he could see was these women he'd made up. Well, I helped. So the girls, not the manatees, took him back to the Royal Crown and deposited him in his bed. They left wet towels all over the place and a couple of strategically placed sequins. He'll wonder about that deal the rest of his life. He thinks these babes are fifty or sixty, hell, they're 300 if they're a day.

Ripped, though, and built. Not like some of those 300-year-olds, all dried elephant skin and skulls. Please. I'm out to attract prospects, not scare the daylights out of them. Not for openers anyway. Merilee's extensions cost a thousand bucks a session. Four or five times a year. Brother.

So, Jake gets up, stretches, scratches, goes to the bathroom. In there, he looks in the full-length mirror, likes what he sees, notices a little gleam in the mirror from his nether region. I like saying that. He turns again, it gleams. He looks down, finds a beige sequin on his testicle sac. He puts it on the sink and tries to get his mind around it. Then he notices all the wet towels piled up in the bathroom. Like a bunch of people came in from a swimming party and dried off. He frowns in deep thought. Nah, that was a dream. This can be explained. Then he returns to the bedroom, selects some clothes to wear to the car show/ carnival/benefit, spies another sequin on the bed. He picks that up, studies it, places it next to the one on the sink. Frowns again.

The girls left a whiff of something like Scheherazade and ozone on the towels, which puzzles him—*they should smell like chlorine*, he's thinking. There's lipstick, just a trace, on one of them. He shakes his head, runs a shower until it's right, and climbs in.

In the steam on the mirror, I wrote *XXX, M,L,&N*. I was just jacking with him. I get bored. I'll probably leave him pretty much alone, I mean he already drank and smoked and those unnatural acts with manatees, how weird is that? This guy would be along if left to his own devices. Merilee was my best soulsucker, and I almost had her do a succubus number on him, but put it back into him with some air while he was playing synchronized swimmer. You humans are such dorks. Well, I can't exactly speak for them all, just sometimes.

Out of the shower, Jake used one of the damp towels that smelled faintly of exotic perfume and saw what looked like writing on the mirror, but it faded quickly. He breathed on it, but to no avail.

He pulled on his ostrich-skin boots, tucked a starched white shirt into his Wranglers, and grabbed a khaki sport coat, holding it over one shoulder with two fingers, stopped by the full-length mirror, smiled. It was a good look. His bull-riding buckle caught the light, and he thought of the sequins. He began to bulge beneath the buckle when the dream came back to him. He cleared his throat and thought of other things, like where were his keys?

At the desk, he said he wouldn't be checking out at noon and would like another day. The gnome-like clerk wore a tuxedo coat with tails and glasses that looked surprisingly like marrow bones with orange lenses in them. "Any, uhh, messages?" Jake asked.

"This ain't the Four Seasons, pal. Oh, pardon *moi*, I forget myself, *oui*, there *ees thees for m'sieu*," and he handed Jake a small envelope.

Jake glanced at the strange little man's name tag: Dante LeMac. LeMac stirred something in his memory pan. He opened the envelope. *Wonderful night. Wet and wild. See you at the fair?* No signature, but three lipstick kisses. Perfumed. When he looked up, the clerk was gone. Wet and wild. Could mean the many drinks. Could mean they all got wet—and wild. He shoved the note and envelope into his back pocket and walked to the pool. The padlocked gate's sign said Pool Open at Noon, No Lifeguard. The turquoise water lapped at the sides lightly.

He entered the lobby, approached a continental breakfast bar, and poured himself a cup of coffee. Glancing over at RC's Oasis, he did a mild double take—the sign now said *Chez Zahara*. The doors were boarded shut and a placard said Closed for Remodeling. When he cupped his hands around his eyes to look through the glass, he saw it was bare inside other than some wiring sticking out of the floor and a stack of sheetrock.

"Closed since last month, sorry."

Startled, he turned to face a girl dressed in a motel uniform. Very attractive but odd, somehow.

"Closed? But I—"

"Yes?" Wide-eyed, innocent look, but also wise. Old. She looked old if he didn't look right at her. About eighteen, otherwise.

"Nothing." This was nuts, he thought. "Is there a singing group performing at the motel at night?"

She snickered. "Well, they say there was a group

singing in your room last night, so maybe that counts. We got some complaints."

"What?"

"You use an incredible amount of towels. There's extra charges for that."

He glanced at her name tag. Rhonda LeMac.

"Can I ask you a personal question, Rhonda? You any relation to Dante LeMac?"

"Never heard of him."

"Gotta run. See you, Rhonda."

And he did. Run. He could have sworn he heard her call after him, "Just fuckin' witcha."

When he drove by, he glimpsed the bar as it was the night before. Must be something he drank.

The fairgrounds were humming. He parked in the grass and walked to the camel raffle. Easy to find, groaning camel, yappy little blue heeler mix dog, some shriners.

"What's the matter with that camel?" he asked a portly fez-wearing gentleman. The man looked like Sidney Greenstreet in *The Maltese Falcon*.

"I assure you, young man, that camel is in the peak of his few years, absolutely top condition. Camels are merely vocal, sir. He comes with a trailer that has electric brakes, and this fine loading dog as well."

He *talked* like Sidney Greenstreet. Where was Peter Lorre? Jake wondered. Synaptically, he saw him in the crowd, fez, tails, marrow-bone glasses. Jake wasn't surprised. Whatever it was would work out of his system he was sure, maybe it had been acid. Probably was. Those rascally beautiful sisters.

He reached his hand out to the dog, got bitten immediately.

"Shit!" he shook his hand, pulled a handkerchief from his breast pocket, and wrapped it around his bleeding finger.

"Yes," said Greenstreet, "the pup lacks restraint, but load he will. You'll delight in his skills at getting this big fellow aboard the trailer. It seems to be what he lives for."

"You can keep the fice dog," said a voice behind Jake. "I'd sooner have a pet snake than that mean little sumbitch. Actually, you can keep the camel too. I just want the trailer." A man in a cowboy hat handed the Shriner a five-dollar bill and took a raffle ticket, wrote laboriously on it, and deposited it in a big pickle jar.

Greenstreet shook with silent laughter as he put the money in a cashbox. Jake gave him his five, and put his ticket in the jar. He walked to a faux French outdoor Café, ordered a sandwich and a beer, and watched the crowd eddying by.

The sign above him said *Chameau* and was illustrated with a camel, palm trees, and pyramids. A voice from the passersby chimed, "Well look who's here!"

It was Merrilee, and her sisters, all decked out in fancy desert togs, cargo shorts, loose linen blouses, hiking boots, and camo tennis shoes. One had a boonie hat,

Merrilee wore a tennis visor, and the other had on a linen newsboy cap. They were a-jangle with bracelets and jewelry, tanned and sexy, eyes glittering. He was delighted to see them, the feeling they may have experienced four-way sex stronger than the desire to chide them for drugging him. If, indeed, either had been the case. Great legs, anyway.

They clattered into chairs around his table and ordered drinks while he ate his sandwich. Nancy hummed and drummed on the table with her fingers, "The Campbells Are Coming, da dump, bump, bump."

Louise said, "So, Jake, was it a night well spent?"

Merrilee snorted into her umbrella drink then sucked on it with a straw. She placed a tanned leg over one of his and moved closer so her ample chest was resting on his arm.

"I'm not sure. You tell me."

"Are we so forgettable?"

The sisters launched into an a cappella version of "Unforgettable," segueing into "My Funny Valentine," to the scattered applause and laughter from the tables around them. Merilee squeezed his thigh.

"All so banal," said the man in the marrow-bone glasses.

"When are you going home, Jake?" asked Merrilee.

"Tomorrow, if I win the camel. Tonight, if I don't. I'll need to acquaint myself with the big fella and get him a good night's rest before we—"

"Well, come by the Chez Zahara, then, for a special show."

"RC's Oasis, you mean?"

"What. Ever," said Nancy. She brightened, "Want to go to the freak tent?"

"You guys go without me. We'll meet up at the bumper cars, okay?"

There was, of course, no freak tent. He knew that. But had he gone with them, one would have materialized, seriously freakish. But those *legs*. And the linen tops that swung about with such interesting unfettered cargo. *Maaaannnn*, he thought. *I want to stay so badly. I want them in the worst way. But if I stay, maybe that's how I'll get them. Yikes.* He returned, with some regret, to his truck. And he awoke, trying to recall some dream about blue water and graceful swimmers.

ပာပာ

As I checked out that morning, I felt invigorated. Crystal clear day, crisp fall temperature. I should be in Oklahoma City by late afternoon. Snatches of dream kept bumping into my consciousness, graceful women in water, a crowded midway, songs from my youth. I tried to bring it all up, but it disappeared in the smoke of memory. A small, but robust, tribe in the Amazon believe that dreams are our real lives, and our "waking hours" are but a dream. The dreams of our real lives guide us through the days. Others talk of parallel lives, barely remembered through the gauzy wall of sleep and waking.

"Sir?" The desk clerk's voice brought me out of the reverie. "I asked if you used the phone this morning. Any long distance?"

"No, none. Sorry."

She smiled and took my card, prepared a bill which I signed.

"Thanks for staying with Fairfax Inns. Have a safe trip. Oh, darn…" She bit her lip and looked toward the door.

I followed her glance and saw a sort of blue-heeler-mix dog trot through the door with a woman who had just driven up.

"He just came in when I did," the woman said, "I couldn't stop him."

"I know," said the desk clerk. "Some people dumped her out in the lot a couple of days ago. She keeps coming in, looking at the guests, trying to find her family, I think. It's so sad."

I said, "You know, I'm almost home. I could take her and maybe keep her. I'll be living rural, and she'd have good home. That is, if she's friendly."

"Oh, she's a sweetheart. We shouldn't have but we gave her scraps and now we're her base of operations. Poor thing."

I hunkered down, called the dog. She came right over, wagging her stump tail. I checked her over for wounds, fleas, her teats were full, pregnant—no doubt why the people dumped her. I'd have to get her spayed after the pups came. Get her shots. She'd be okay for the trip to Oklahoma City. Until I found a place, she could stay at the vet's kennel. One I knew would take good care of her.

The desk clerk was clearly relieved. She came out around the partition, gathered her skirt, and hunkered down to pat the dog. She reminded me of a girl I knew from Dalhart, great smile. And other things.

"We'll miss you, hon," she said as she ruffled the dog's ears. "What'll you name her?" She looked up at me, brightly.

"What town are we in?"

"Campbell, Texas," she said proudly.

"Campbell it is."

"Cammy for short."

"Deal. I'm outa here, me and my dog, Cammy. Dogs. She's preggers."

"They'll be so cute. Send me pictures." She handed me a card which read *Merrilee Burnette, Customer Service, Fairfax Inns International.*

I did that.

That was over twenty years ago, before email, before the proliferation of cellphones and instant communication. Merrilee and I wrote often and we saw each other after I settled down on 100-plus acres and built a place. Cammy was some kind of fine dog, worked cows like she was trained to it. Her offspring were not as adept, but good dogs, all. Three horses have died of old age on my place since then. Cam is long gone. Merilee and I quit smoking the same week about eighteen years ago. We get along pretty damn good. Her mom comes to visit now and then. Her mom and her two aunts, her mom's sisters, used to be mermaids at Weeki Wachee Springs, Florida. Lookers, too, from the old photos. Merilee's after us to build a pool.

I even had a crazy dream about it the other night. But the pool was in a desert, and there were camels around it.

WING WALKER

I'd had a librarian fantasy since I was a sophomore in high school, and I'd watched Mrs. Limbaugh walk between the tall shelves with her cart, replacing books when she didn't have a couple of girls helping her. When she reached up high and stood on her toes, you could kind of see her butt muscles flex, and her blouse tighten over her bra. She wore skirts like the girls did, pencil skirts they called them, and, in my mind, her nylons whispered to me as she walked briskly back and forth.

Sometimes when her excused-from-gym girl helpers were with her, they'd all be in the back shelves and they'd break out in quiet snuffling laughter, the kind that said what we're laughing about is maybe dirty or sexy.

I had her sign her picture in my yearbook when I graduated last May. She seemed surprised and asked my name. I thought she knew it. Anyway, she wore tortoiseshell-rimmed glasses on a chain and she moved in a way that compelled watching. So I had a librarian fantasy like a lot of guys, and also a Catholic girl in plaid skirt fantasy after older guys told me about them. But all fantasies were replaced by an aerial photographer fantasy. And all others forever dimmed.

I lived on my dad's farm right now. Sort of a temporary caretaker. I used to live here as a kid. My mom had moved back to the city, when I was little. She took me with her. My dad came, too, later. I don't really remember much about it. I had some ducks when we all lived on the farm. She named them Fubar and Snafu, I remember that. Which I found out what that means, so I guess what I'm telling next is probably true.

My old man and I were out at the farm, checking pipes and closing it up for winter, talking, and he said my mom said, "Fuck this hayseed life, it's not for me." And she moved. I asked him, was that *actually* what she said, and he said, "Word for word. I swear it." And he laughed. "But don't ever tell her I told you that." I gulped and tried to picture my mom saying it but could only see a cartoon of her that looked like Blondie, and a thought balloon that said those words. I felt guilty seeing even that. I'd had fantasies about Blondie earlier in my life.

Anyway, I was taking a year off before college, and making my '42 Ford the fastest car in the western free non-commie world, as my old man said, then I'd go to college in 1959, driving my fast car. It was in the barn and I was almost done putting a '57 Canadian Ford truck engine in it, bored 80 over, Iskendarian cam, to replace the old vapor-locking flathead, and once that was done, then I was really getting down to business. Heads. Carbs. Mallory Ignition. Quick change rear end. Pipes with cutouts you could pull at the dash. It was lowered and painted a bright magenta, but that might change.

The other day at a stop light an old fart in a Plymouth said, "Looks like a Easter egg," and cackled.

It was sort of bulbous and maybe even egg-shaped with that round ass end. But it was classic. Like I said, maybe I'd paint it primer, and with a hood scoop on it, it wouldn't look like any Easter egg. Maybe I was too sensitive. Old guys should just shut the fuck up in my opinion. Or impart great wisdom. Which I was seeing that fewer and fewer old guys had any.

So, the farm. I guess it was maybe forty-plus acres. The old man was never a farmer, said he couldn't stand the hours and laughed. He just had the idea he wanted to live away from the city, and he did for a while. The house was small, old, propane for heat, front porch sagged, new roof. Old one leaked too bad. Nice barn with a chain hoist and strong rail for the pulley. Couple sheds. Overgrown fields where someone once grew soybeans, now home to a lot of doves, quail, turkeys. The old man brought a dog out and hunted in the fall. Rip was our German Shorthair pointer, pretty old, but still loved the fields.

I liked it out here when the weather was good, but it

was too hot and too cold otherwise. There was no real caretaker work for me to do here, except the painting— and that's how I financed my coupe.

This summer I was painting the house, barn, and outbuildings. My folks were going to sell the place. So it wasn't like I was a real caretaker. No livestock, no tractor, a rickety riding mower that I trimmed the lawn with— and the "lawn" was wherever I wanted it to be, around the house. I did insulate the north wall down by the pipes, dry-walled the bedroom. Coyotes raised hell at dusk and early morning. And I could understand why my mom got out, sure could.

I could drink beer here, and smoke, maybe could at home too, but I didn't know that. And I read a lot. Listened to records on a 33 they got me for my birthday. There was a TV that worked sometimes, black and white, I watched Dragnet when it was on and the rabbit ears worked. It was kind of like an odd vacation—lonely, but I had my car to work on, and the desire to get it running again so I could get away from here nights when I felt like it. I painted most mornings. No hurry on that. I had all summer. The scraping was the worst part and it was almost all done. The painting was mindless, okay work. Under the eaves, I had to get the wasp's nests out, but otherwise okay.

I was having a beer on the front porch, feet up on the railing, sitting in an old kitchen chair rocked back on its hind two legs, when a plane went over low. Really low. I stood, looked up, as a great-looking little piston aircraft, a colorful red and yellow biplane, looked like a stunt plane, or one of those racer planes, flew over the house, then climbed and turned, came back over the main pasture, turned again, flew over the barn. Whoever was flying it seemed preoccupied with the little farm, and made more passes over it. I took a leak over the railing while watching it. Finally it flew away. I sat back down, forgot about it. I had one of the more dramatic records on the player, *Victory at Sea*, something my mom bought with the stereo, and I did kind of like it. It was on loud inside the house, so I could hear it on the porch. It was a long-play album, and I smoked and drank while it boomed movie-type music out into the yard. I felt pretty good, what with the beer buzz and the plane and the symphonic crash of the music. I waved my arms like a conductor and whirled about on the porch. The buzz was sharp-edged and perfect, and so was I.

When the buzz died down, I felt a little guilty, because my coupe was sitting in the barn, drive shaft laying in the dirt, waiting for me to tighten down the motor mounts, hook that Canadian Ford up to it. It wasn't getting done this way. And I'd be itching to get to town sometime soon. There was a lot of grunt work to do just to get it running and I was lazy some days. I wanted to get the painting done before it got too hot out here—getting a pretty good tan as it was.

A week or two later, the coupe was sitting out front,

the barn was mostly painted, and I was on the porch again with a beer, *Victory at Sea* booming away inside. I needed to get more records but I didn't have money for stuff other than the car and groceries right now. But, this was the life, I was thinking, when a car turned into the gravel drive, crunching to a stop behind the coupe.

It was a 1956 Ford two-toned, black and white, hard top convertible they called them, even though the top didn't go down. It had minimum pillars, and this one had a plexiglas half-top from the front to midway back on the roof. Pretty snazzy looking car. A woman was behind the wheel. She waved and started rummaging around on the back seat for something. I saw she was wearing shorts, since her rear end was all that was visible for a moment, until she found what she was searching for. I stood up, put my beer down, and walked halfway out there. I had on a pair of cutoff jeans and some sneakers, was all, but it was my house, so to speak. I didn't dress for company. When she got out of the car, I saw she was about twenty-five and good-looking. Really good-looking. Sleeveless blouse, shorts, and those ballet type shoes the girls all wore. Her hair was black, in a pageboy, eyes green, skin kind of olive like Italian or something. She was gorgeous. Like Elizabeth Taylor. Movie gorgeous.

She walked right up to where I was standing, carrying a large envelope, some papers, and a framed picture, maybe one foot by two foot. I stood with my hands in my front pockets.

She looked around, gestured with the big envelope. "This your place?"

"Sort of—" I started to explain, but she went on.

"Want to see some pictures of it?"

"Sure," I said. "Come on up to the porch." I moved a wicker table and another chair over by mine, picked up my beer from the railing. I held it up, said, "Want a beer? Or ice water, or a Coke, or something?"

She sat in the chair and laid the picture face down on the table, put the other stuff on it. "Love a beer, thanks."

From inside, I noticed she looked at her face in a mirror compact, snapped it shut, and put it back in a little clutch purse she'd brought up with her. Then she took ahold of the front of her sleeveless blouse and fluttered it as though it might be sticking to her.

"Thanks. What's that music?" she asked, when I handed her a cold beer.

"*Victory at Sea*," I said.

"Beautiful." She took a sip of the beer. "I'm Nancy Graves. Aerial photographer." She handed me a card she must have taken from her purse with the compact.

I held it, studied it, said, "Billy, uh Bill Altaire."

She put out her hand, I shook it, and we held hands like that for a little bit. Seemed right.

"Nice to meet you, Bill."

Something about the combination of her bright eyes, and the quickness of her smile to come and go, unsettled me some. And she kept shaking her head, as though trying to get rid of a thought, or summon one up.

"Pictures," she said, and our hands fell apart.

Suddenly it clicked, the little sport biplane, that was
what it was doing, taking pictures. She opened the envelope and spilled some photos out on the wicker table.
Some fell on the floor and we both went after them at the
same time which occasioned me to bump my head on
hers and also get a quick flash of breasts under her shirt.
Her hair smelled like barroom smoke and soap. I sensed
time slowing to a crawl. We laughed. I felt some heat in
my face and elsewhere.

The pictures were sharp. There was the barn. The
fields, neatly bordered by tree line and old fence. The
outbuildings. A longer shot with the county roads criss-
crossing. The house. Me peeing off the porch. I took that
one and examined it closely.

"You took these?"

"I took 'em."

"Who flew the plane?"

"Me. I'm quick and I'm good. I have a blowup of
you. Your stream needs to be more clear. You should
drink more water during the day. All people should, but
nobody really knows that."

How intimate, I thought. We could be a married couple. *My stream.*

"What kind of plane is that?"

"Old Stearman crop duster, but it's been souped up
plenty. Pratt and Whitney R-985, constant speed prop.

Custom paint. Rehabbed prop to tail. I race, powder puff. Aerobatics. I wing walk. I did it naked in Iowa and got banned. Which was silly, because no one could really see me, but the girl flying it."

I looked at her. I could see her naked on the wide wing, leaning into the wind. Man, oh, man, oh, Maneshcevitz, as my old man would say. It was a wine slogan.

"Do you hold on to anything?"

"With my feet. Couple straps up there. I don't actually walk, except getting up there."

"Then you're a hood ornament, sort of," I said.

"Yeah, exactly! Rolls Royce. That's me."

She laughed and leaned forward, breasts out, head up, hands at her sides. I was deeply in love. For an anniversary, I would give her a gold-plated Rolls hood ornament. I would learn to fly immediately. I would sell my coupe, my soul, for the lessons. I was jittery. My coupe? Jeezo, what was going on here?

"You like the pictures?" Her question brought me back.

"Yeah, I do. But the owner is going to sell this place so, I don't think—"

"Better yet," she said. "Pictures like these are a great vehicle for selling, shows people what they're getting in a view few ever see."

"Well—"

"Ask the owner. Show him. He can have these for less than a hundred bucks. I'll make him a deal."

"That's pretty expensive for an old farmhouse."

"Okay," she said, looking a little miffed. "I'll sell him the whole thing for fifty bucks. And that includes the framed picture of the farmhouse and surrounding area..."

She drained about half her beer then arranged the pictures on the floor in sections, changing one with another like a deck of cards in suits. I was entranced, watching her down on all fours, then up, then down on one knee.

She propped the framed picture on the floor against the table at the top of the arrangement, slid her hands against one and another a couple times, looked at me. "Well? Aren't you going to look at them?"

She had a leaf on one knee from the porch floor. I wanted to carry her off. I hunkered down, looking from one photo to another.

"Now those are just crappy prints on cheap paper. The real ones will be like photos you see in the drugstore."

"They look pretty good to me. Must be hard steering and taking pictures."

"There's a trick to it, all right."

She was standing next to me, bare legs so close I could see the darker pores and texture of her skin, smell her warmth; a mixture of perfume and perspiration, maybe some airplane fuel.

"Well, gotta run, Bill. Tell you what, you sell the owner on these and I'll give you ten bucks commission.

So, forty bucks now, and I'll send you the finished work special delivery. You keep the framed print. How's that?"

When I didn't answer, she said, "The framed print is worth fifty all by itself. My art photos get more than that in a gallery show." She finished her beer and bent over toward me, picking up the prints off the floor. I could see her breasts and I think she knew it. The music from *Victory at Sea* hit a crescendo and she stood suddenly then sort of wavered and dropped all the prints.

She seemed in a trance and started to fall. "I...uh...aahhh..." she said, or something like it, and fell.

I caught her and laid her down on the porch floor where she began to stiffen and thrash some. I knew what it was, I'd seen it in science class in junior high school. Epilepsy. A kid had gone down off his stool and hit the floor during an experiment of some kind. The teacher had quickly put a rolled up cloth in his mouth, crossways, and later told us it was to keep him from biting his tongue. I grabbed some of the proofs and rolled them tightly, but couldn't get her jaw unclenched. Her tongue was inside her teeth so it didn't look like she'd bite it.

I felt helpless. Should I raise her head? Shit, I couldn't remember anything else the science teacher had done, maybe nothing. I couldn't remember. Then she relaxed and her eyes opened. I was conscious of having held my breath for a long time, let out an explosion of air, and said "Oh, God," at the same time.

"What?" she said, confused. "What?" Then she

seemed cold and frightened and held her arms, sat up.

"You had a...I don't know, a sort of...you passed out," I said.

"I have to get out of here," she said. I started to help her up and she scooted back. "Don't!"

I stopped and put my hands up. Maybe she thought I'd messed with her somehow. Maybe she thought the beer was spiked or something.

She relaxed some. "I'll be all right," she said. "I missed taking a pill, then beer, nothing to eat, and the music, yes the music..."

I hurried inside and turned the stereo off.

She was still hugging herself and sitting on the floor when I came back. "Bells have set me off before, sound stimulus. It's ep—it's a seizure is all, not often, doesn't happen that much."

"Can I get you anything? A cold wet towel?" I thought of her flying and all the stimuluses, stimuli, that could have. Even driving. Then that awful joke came floating into my mind, the one where they tie an epileptic girl to a bed during a fit, and the guy climbs on and says "Okay, cut her loose!" I looked away from her and swallowed. She looked, seemed, so vulnerable. *Forgive me, Lord.* If I ever went to confession again, how many Hail Marys would that be worth?"

"So sound can do this?" I said.

"Only if I'm really, really stupid. Like not taking my medicine. Then not eating. Then drinking alcohol. It takes a number of things. I should have known, I had warning a couple times—"

"Warning?"

"Like mood changes, getting annoyed, weird feeling—for no reason." She sat cross-legged on the floor; I did the same across from her.

"I need to eat something," she said.

I made her a fried egg sandwich and poured some milk that was still good. Or at least not "blinky," as my mom says when she sniffs a turning milk bottle. I toasted the bread as it might be a little stale, then I cut the sandwich in half so it was triangles. My mom stopped by with groceries sometimes, and I drove into town for things. I just hoped she wouldn't show up now. The phone had been disconnected long ago.

Nancy lit a cigarette after eating most of the sandwich and we talked for a long time at the kitchen table.

႙ჯჀ

In bed, hours later, she said "Billy. You are Billy, not Bill."

"What does that mean?" I said, a little defensively. I rolled over half on top of her, looked into those eyes, saw freckles under them and on her nose I hadn't noticed before.

"It only means Billy is what you are. Bill is anybody. Bill is boring. Be Billy, always."

"All right." I kissed her.

I was a little embarrassed about the state of my room, but at least it was newly drywalled and painted, and it smelled chemical and clean. I hoped those weren't stimuli.

I was glad I wasn't a virgin, but we also did things I hadn't done before, only heard about. They seemed to come quite naturally.

❧❧❧

She wouldn't tell me where she lived, but she let me come to the little airport where she kept Byrd, the biplane, on Wednesdays. The mechanics at the county airport liked the coupe, and the color, too. When I first showed up out there, two of them, Herschel and Ike, came over and asked questions about it. Johnson County wasn't developed back then, and they called the airport Plowed Ground. The farm was even farther out than the airport. I had to drive my coupe over gravel roads to get there and picked up new rattles with each trip, so I didn't just drive out there, unless I was pretty sure she'd be there.

I found out she was the daughter of some big shot at Boeing over in Wichita, that he'd bought her the car, but didn't like her flying.

I'd paid for the pictures out of my painting money, we agreed on thirty bucks, and hadn't showed them to my dad yet, although I'd had the chance when he came out to

look at the progress. Trouble is, the pictures of the buildings had a patchwork look being in the middle of painting
and scraping. Nancy said she'd come back and shoot it
again for free. Then I could sell him those. Luckily, he'd
fronted me some more money, but not enough for supplies and the high compression heads I wanted. They
could wait. A man has to eat, smoke, drink beer, buy
fresh milk.

Up on the ladder, painting, I had a patch left about
six foot by ten foot on the barn and I'd be done with it. A
plane flew over, high, not Nancy, but the sound of it
buzzing along in the almost cloudless blue sky pulled at
my heart. I finished up and tapped the lid onto the paint
can, squirting red paint onto my sneaker. I washed the
brush out at the pump hydrant and laid it on the can,
washed myself off at the hydrant naked. I walked around
in nothing but my sneakers to dry off in the sun, thinking
you couldn't do this in the city.

Then I gathered up my shorts and underwear, went to
the house like that. I put on *Victory at Sea* and got a hard-
on. Stimulus. Nancy and *Victory at Sea*. I danced around
the kitchen, into the tiny parlor. A horn honked out front.
My mom. She never honked—oh shit, she must have
seen me, gone back to the car. I hopped around trying to
get my shorts on, fell over. Fuck! I didn't think I had the
boner when I danced into the front of the house. But I
was naked.

After managing to get my shorts on, I went out on

the porch and waved at her, walked to the car. Casual. Red-faced, I could feel it. She was opening the trunk. Maybe she hadn't seen me.

"Brought you some groceries, hon. And some frozen TV Dinners in a cooler. I hope there's room in the little freezer in that old fridge." She handed me a bag and opened the cooler, took out a little stack of flat packages.

We had to chip the ice out of the freezer compartment with a hammer and screwdriver, but we got the packages in there, cleaned up the mess.

"You need some dish towels," she said, eyeing the sink. "Do you *ever* wash dishes?"

"Sure. You just caught me at a bad time, Mom."

That's when she exploded with laughter, like she'd been holding it in. "I know, Nature Boy. Farm life seems to appeal to you." Then she kissed my flaming-red face, held it with both hands. "Oh, Billy," she said and laughed some more. "I'm not laughing at you, I'm…laughing at you!" And she laughed again, high-tinkling laughter, the kind that makes others laugh, wiping laugh tears away.

I started laughing, too. God, I was embarrassed. We sort of hugged, hiding our embarrassment, shaking still.

❧❧❧

Wednesday dawned a good clear picture morning so I knew she'd be out at the airport getting her plane ready. The coupe was running good and I'd de-rattled all the little rattling places with shims and tightening. I started it and listened to the pipes, revved it and heard the air rushing into the little air cleaner on top of the quad carb. The Smitty mufflers popped when I let off the gas. "Ready fucking teddy," I shouted and threw gravel as I pulled out, turning the radio on in the middle of "It's Only Make Believe" by Conway Twitty. I turned it up, sang along, and goosed the coupe when I got to the asphalt.

I saw Herschel and Ike in their gray coveralls, talking to a cop, next to a Johnson County Sheriff's Patrol car. Nancy's Ford was parked by the hangar where she kept Byrd. I waved at Herschel who looked at me, then down at the ground, not waving back. I parked by Nancy's car. The dark hangar housed two other small planes but hers was gone. I walked back out into the sun, saw the three men coming toward me. I knew then.

I could tell it this way. I could say I was numb and didn't run back into the hangar and slide the big doors shut, and run to the man-door and try to lock it before they forced their way in. I could say I didn't shout and scream and evade their clutches and whirl and yell "Fuck you!" and "Shut up, shut up, shut up!" and kick and throw anything I could find at them before I was subdued. I could say I experienced all the predictable stages of grief in the following months and understood them all. I could even say Nancy had a seizure before she "augured in," as Herschel put it, without meaning to be ironic or cruel at all. He was just an air guy. It was how they talked.

I could say time had softened the edges of memory and that I didn't first think of the freckles on her nose, and then her breasts, when I thought of her. I never thought of where we were going, I just waited for Wednesdays or the odd day that she'd show up in the driveway of the old farmhouse. I knew she had a real life. I didn't know she was getting married to someone her old man approved.

What I know: she wing walked on the top wing of a co-pilotless biplane on a beautiful sunny cloudless Wednesday, and she wore a wedding dress as she stood, arms at her sides, leaning into the wind.

THE PERFORMANCE

They come in twos and threes, quietly, like Sioux to a sweat lodge that is unannounced. They just know, so they come, mostly elders. Some are younger, all white men, wind and sun and past pains show in their faces—farmers, some are factory workers, a mechanic, a housepainter. The younger ones have connected with one another by cellphone. A dozen or so in all. They stand silently, waiting, by the old man's barn. One of the younger ones starts to talk facetiously and is hushed by an elder. He tugs at his ball cap bill, shoves his hands into the pockets of his frayed canvas chore coat, hunches against the cold, eyes to the ground.

The old man emerges from his weathered shotgun house. Only the outbuildings show any sign of recent care. He wears a long camelhair polo coat, belted in back, high collar, wide lapels. It is either highly fashionable or quite old, but looks new. He takes no notice of the group as he approaches the barn. A few inches of striped overalls show beneath the voluminous coat, the kind railroad workers used to wear. Well-worn, expensive workboots. His billed cap says Millett with a crosshair and Tactical beneath that. His eyes are expressionless.

They say he's a witch. Not your Wiccan, new-age type, but the kind who can be standing near you in his old rusty pipe corral then suddenly fifty feet away on the peak of his barn, looking down, his odd coat ballooning out at the skirts in the wind. You felt a loss of time then, the air smelled like a storm, and the hairs on your neck rose. They rise now when you think of it. You wonder if it happened at all.

He approaches the barn, eyes in triangular shadows under the bill of his cap. On the side of the barn is a worn spot in the red paint about three feet from the ground and some two feet in diameter. This is where the ball hits when he does what they've come and gathered quietly to see.

He stands in front of the spot, gazing at it. The wind kicks up and the sawgrass around his boots bends to the east. A plastic Seven-Eleven bag frees itself from some thistle in the pasture and dances toward the pond and surrounding woods.

He pulls a lavender colored bag from inside his coat. It looks like a makeup bag his wife might use. He unzips it and takes one of several tennis balls from it, tosses the bag aside. The green tennis ball he holds is worn and faded. He holds it in both hands now, like a pitcher before windup. He is about five feet from the barn. He throws the ball at the weathered spot and catches it as it bounces back, throws again, catches again, *ponk-pup, ponk-pup*. He throws faster and faster and the sounds begin to merge and smooth into small motor noise, and the old man whirls in place, perhaps levitates, one can't be sure, and the ball may bounce off his blurred boots at times. He is connected to the barn by the ball's energy, but now it's all too fast to comprehend.

The *thing*, the…performance, is over. The old man stoops to pick up the lavender bag, drops the ball inside, zips it, and, without acknowledging the group, walks away toward the gray weathered house. The small group disperses, as quietly as they'd arrived, to their pickups and battered cars with different colored fenders and doors.

℘ℑ℘

A silver Audi coupe pulls up in a swirl of gravel dust. Both doors open and two young men emerge, leaving the doors ajar. The man on the passenger side wears jeans and a hooded sweatshirt, and he is doing something with a video camera. The other man is in a sport coat and tie, and he hurries toward the old man with a microphone and a battery pack.

"Sir! Sir! Mr. Beels! We're from KSTV and—" he yells, with a smile on his face.

The old man turns to them as the cameraman catches up and aims the camera at him. The old man, still expressionless, produces an antique-looking small-caliber revolver—possibly a .32—and points it in their direction. A shot snaps and the lens of the camera explodes.

The loose group of men who had come to watch the earlier performance are frozen in attitude, one holding a lit lighter, a cigarette stuck to his lower lip, mouth open.

"Get out of range," the old man says. "I'll count ten. One…two…"

The two men bolt for the Audi, and it wheels about in the gravel, one door still open, the cameraman grabbing at it to close it. Three shots. Three dents appear in the license plate. The old man resumes walking to his house.

The other trucks and cars pull out slowly, some with turn signals flashing as they turn onto the road that brought them there.

MIDNIGHT ROBOT

The line shack was essentially his in 1984. Old man Hawthorne told him so. Harold Lujack had a place to call his own, finally. The Hawthorne place, the Circle H, was owned by fifth-generation ranch people and run pretty much as it had been in 1918 by Tom Hawthorne. Section after section of rich west Nebraska land. You could ride for ten miles before you had to open a gate. Then another ten. It never stopped until the Wyoming line, Harold marveled.

Harold was a good hand and had earned his spot on the Circle H. Now he felt settled at fifty-seven. He had health insurance, a place to live, a good horse, and a remuda string of backups. What more could a cowhand want? The shelves were full of old pulp westerns and science fiction books from the 1940s, and he'd read them all once, some twice.

Harold's robot stood in the corner of the shack. He'd

won it in a card game at a truck stop in Grand Island when the old man who'd lost the hand emptied his pockets and was eighty bucks short. Lucky for him, Harold liked robots. And this wasn't some cheap Toys-R-Us robot. It looked like the ones in his Buck Rogers books.

Robot was the main decoration in the plain chinked-log shack, the only other being a faded girlie wall calendar from the forties.

Harold held conversations with both.

Cabin fever came on suddenly this Nebraska winter, the coldest winter in twenty years, and he'd been socked in, running low on everything, including books, booze, and firewood. Out of hay, he turned the horses loose to find their way back to the Circle H, and he turned in, the last thing on his mind before sleep, the summers of his youth.

Some trick of the atmosphere had gotten the robot running, whirring, at night. Midnight was pitch black until the robot started moving a little on the hardwood floor, ran into a deer hide throw, and started turning in place, casting a weird red light beam around and around.

Harold awoke, covers up around his nose, "What th—what are you supposed to be, a fuckin' lighthouse?"

"Well, if it ain't Ned the cowboy," the thing answered in a voice unused to talking, scratchy, fragile.

"Don't call me that, dammit to hail. I'm a buckaroo. Harold Lujack. By gol, I'll come over there and short your circuits—"

"Bring it, Fuckaroo." The voice gaining strength, resonance.

"What! What was that?!"

"Buckaroo, I said. Bring a bag lunch and a John Deere tractor, you gone fuck with me."

Harold kicked the striped Hudson's Bay wool blankets off, put his feet on the cold floor, and grabbed his gun belt from the bedpost, strapped it on over his long johns. He pulled his boots on, all the while watching the robot with wary eyes, his lower jaw thrust out in defiance.

"True grit," said the robot.

A taunt, it seemed to Harold. Then it scooted about on the wood floor, whirling wildly, singing a Men Without Hats song about dancing if you wanted to.

"That's the limit," Harold said, as he drew the big hog-leg .44, and fanned off five shots in the robot's direction. One of the slugs ricocheted off the robot's steel tummy and whizzed into Lujack's forehead. He heard it coming but couldn't duck in time. Sounded like a hornet. Felt like a hammer.

"That's gonna smell some come springtime. Good thing I don't get all olfactory," Robot said. He motored over to Lujack. "I see by your outfit, that you are a cowboy." Then he laughed so hard he blew a fuse.

In spring, they found Lujack's bones, a neat hole in the middle of his skull, and his shelf full of old science fiction books.

"Looks like he couldn't take it. Shot the place up

then turned the gun on hisself," said Hawthorne's foreman.

"Lookit all these robot books, will you? Just sci-fi
and beef jerky and booze would make anyone crazy, all
shut up like this," Hawthorne said. "Air this place out for
a couple days. Whooo-eee. And get rid of this thing." He
jerked a thumb at the robot.

JESUS RUST

The reason their mailbox was down was that it developed a rust spot on the back, right where the pressed metal says *Steel City Mfg, Youngstown, O.*

Francine didn't want it to rust any more because she saw the face of Jesus in it and, oxidation being unpredictable, it might turn into something else.

"Yeah," Rex said, from the recliner. "It might spread and be Richard Nixon or something and how would you get on *Good Morning America* with that?"

"I don't want to be on *Good Morning America*, smartass. Have you taken a good look at this?" She held it in front of his face.

"I'll look at it after the game, Francine. Get the damn thing down out of my face. Aww, look, I missed the play."

"They'll show it again," she said.

"It's not the same as seeing it when it happens."

She went outside to wait for the post lady, Tiffany. If Francine wasn't right there, now the mailbox was down, Tiffany would pass them up. Francine glanced up at the sky. Looked like snow again.

Tiffany drove up in her Jeep Cherokee with the steering wheel thing on the right. "Hi, Francine. You'll have to get a proper mailbox up or come get your mail at the post office. They won't let me bring it anymore after today." She handed Francine a couple of bills, a Land's End catalog and the *Rolling Stone*.

"I'll get a new one today, Tiffany. Thanks."

"Ace Hardware has 'em. Can I see the old one? I heard about it."

"Sure, pull in the drive. I'll run and get it."

Rex held the box, studying it. "This blob is Jesus?"

"Everyone else can see it. Here, I want to show it to Tiffany." She took it from him and started toward the door.

"Could be they're just being nice, Francine. They might think you've lost it."

"Could be you're an unbeliever, Rex."

"Graven images. Mailbox worship. Not my deal." He turned the sound up on the game.

She held the box so Tiffany could see it, and watched her face for the recognition. It didn't come. Francine held the box sideways, pointed to the eyes. "This is the eyes? See? Here's the beard."

"Oh, now I see it, you've got to look at it awhile, like those puzzle pictures. Wow. Yes. Well, got to run, hon, mail to deliver."

The Jeep made a knocking noise as it took off. Francine looked at the rust spot. It hadn't changed but it was not as convincing as before, when the sun shone on it and she'd seen it in a dizzying moment of exaltation.

The pastor called it pareidolia and had to print it out for her. "It's the tendency to see faces or objects in indistinct shapes. I should think a good many artists have this affliction. Well, maybe not an affliction, just an unusual way to see things." Then he talked about the grilled cheese sandwich on eBay that looked like the Virgin Mary.

"So you think I should eBay this?"

He laughed. "Sure. Or reinstall it so you can get mail."

Francine decided to tell no one about the baking potato that was the spitting image of Jay Leno.

Fuck it. Their loss. But maybe I'll start painting again. Clouds that are things. Vegetable people. Jesus with Steel City across his rusty brow.

TRAIN TIME

Duluth in the 1950s. You don't want to be a drinker in Duluth. Oh, there's plenty of booze, cheap bars, but the hangovers are worse there than any other scrub-ass town on Earth. Even Madill, Oklahoma. Something about the ozone or the devil-chased molecules or some shit. Depressing. An Edward Hopper painting of a life. You drink draw beers and twenty-five-cent shots from some lower-tiered bottle of Colonel Somebody and think about the days until leaving, the days until you board the train to Kansas City.

You've saved up a pile even with the nightly boozing and keep it in a dopp kit, squeezed-together tens and twenties, and occasional fifties and hundreds from the three crap games you'd win big at, and then never played again. That and the steady paycheck from construction of The High Bridge over St. Louis Bay to Superior, Wisconsin. Good money. Plenty of hours, time and a-half, as

they are late on concrete, and even some double time after sixteen hours in any one day. Hard on a laborer, but
you don't have to do it forever, just remember that when
your shoulders ache, your legs tremble, and your biceps
want to seize up.

That dopp kit sits in a rusted shut railroad switching
box on the track nearest the Dago's flophouse, and you
make sure never to approach it or even look that direction
until the residents are snoring or gagging on their own
wine vomit. Four a.m. you wake automatically and trans-
fer more cash to the dopp kit from your workboots which
you sleep in. A rusty safe, that switcher. A panel with
one-inch rusted bolt heads that haven't seen a wrench for
fifty years almost fell off when you tried it. Inside, rusted
relays and corroded wires had been cannibalized and
there's space for that dopp kit. Slap the cover back on,
cock it, and it stays solid even with all the rumbling and
humping of the cars on the labyrinth of nearby tracks that
are still used.

You pay the Dago a dollar a night for a shit room he
calls an apartment with a bed and an old refrigerator that
still works, linoleum floor, and you spray for roaches,
sleep there. No way you try to hide money in there. It
wouldn't last a day. You bitch and moan with the losers
about drinking and gambling your money away, plan a
filling station robbery with a couple of them who
couldn't stick up a Girl Scout selling raffle tickets, and
wait to put this place behind you.

You sleep in a stupor, the switching yard booming and banging all night, cars chunking into one another in a long line of bangs, clanks, ground-shaking ka-booms off into the night. Four a.m. drunk or sober, you throw on a jacket and head down to The Spot, an all-night greasorama that smells of onions and burgers, down a cup of surprisingly good coffee, slow down over the second cup, order eggs, hash browns, steak, ice-cold milk.

Back to the Dago's for S, S, and S. Except you rarely do the third S, and sometimes omit the second. You're not a fucking office worker. You're reminded of this when some stray into your dive, slumming after a party, one or two of the girls laughing too hard and looking like a sailor's wet dream, while the men, young and unsure, try to portray hard guys. You don't bother with any of them, just money down the drain, no future in it, odds of getting laid too long for the work of it.

Finally train day nears. The foreman tells you to go up high. Points you to a bucket of bolts, spud wrench, drift pin. The coffee and eggs try to push up in your throat. This is bad luck, short time and they send you high into the substructure to walk around on three inch angle iron when your nightmare is height, especially height over water.

The week before a man fell onto the steel plate of the barge from eighty feet up. He looked like he'd been in a hay baler.

You say fuck it, walk to the accounting trailer, tell

Slick what's up. He looks at some ledger sheets, makes out your two checks, says, "Where you off to?"

You smile, say, "The Bahamas, where else with money like this?"

You hold the checks up and you both laugh. You can cash the checks in KC at Dave's Stagecoach Inn, pay off your year old tab. Bank the dopp kit stash. Go to farrier school. Welding. Anything but construction. Write a novel like Kerouac. Drive for Red Ball. Go back to art school and be a beatnik.

You're on your own. Three days to train day. You decide to pack anyway, head for the Dago's, do some laundry at the coin-op. There's a crew working close to the wood frame building. They're tearing up track. The switcher is gone! You hurry over there, try to engage the fucking gandy dancer who is pulling spikes with a wheeled machine but he won't look at you. You scan the piles of rusted crap and see the switcher. You drag it to the side and suddenly the crew reacts like bank guards.

One picks up a pry bar and heads toward you. "What are you doing, asshole?"

You hold up your hands. "My old man worked this yard, and it's his birthday. I want to give him this for old time's sake."

He holds the pry bar in a less-menacing way, says, "Ten bucks."

You dig in your jeans, come up with a five and change, offer it. He takes it, shrugs, walks off. You want to kill him. You drag the switcher to the Dago's, dump it on the filthy linoleum floor. Pull the rusty cover. The dopp kit is there. You decide to stay in a hotel until train time.

THE WOMAN WHO LOOKED LIKE LANA TURNER

"Oh, we'll laugh again, we'll just never be young again." ~ Daniel Patrick Moynihan to Mary McGrory at JFK's funeral when she said to him, "We'll never laugh again."

My mother-in-law and I were on the run in 1963.

She looked like Lana Turner. She smoked and drank quite a lot, but her figure was stunning.

My father said of her, "Katherine looks like a Las Vegas showgirl." He also said, "Katherine Riley would be slinging hash in Chicago if it wasn't for Everett."

I doubted that, though Katherine was a little...earthy. A little Mae West. Everett was her husband, my father-in-law, at the time we were on the run. We comprised a glamorous Bonnie and a callow Clyde, thugs of love, drunk on it. But it lasted forty years.

Katherine and I were fond of Everett but our attraction to each other was strong and addictive. I'm sure she loved him, but there was room in her capacity to love me as well. She lived voraciously and loved without hesitation. *All in*, the term for it is these days. We were certainly that.

I'd married Anne in a drunken fog. I was in love with Katherine, but that didn't seem like much of a future, so I settled for Anne. Katherine had put the full court press on me on Anne's behalf when she discovered I was in the Blue Book, the Kansas City Social Register. That made a difference to Katherine, having been poor in childhood, raised in squalor I heard. She was often mistaken for Lana Turner, and there were parallels: Ms. Turner, like Katherine, was the daughter of teenaged parents, and her father was a miner in Appalachia. And, like Lana Turner, she aged well, remaining second-glance beautiful well into her fifties and sixties. I met her in her early forties.

She was Everett's second wife. He'd left a previous family for her. Ev Riley was big, old money, starting with an inherited major brand bottling plant. He'd parlayed that into more millions with Buick/Cadillac dealerships throughout the Midwest.

ↂↂↂ

It was a bit of a shock to all of us when Anne's and my son, Everett Longworth Waller, was born black, nine months after Teddy Blaine, a black friend, had stayed with us on his way to New York to be, as he put it, in legitimate theater. This black kid was supposed to be our firstborn. When we first discovered Anne was pregnant, I just figured the condoms were poor quality. At the hospital birth, I changed that theory to Teddy didn't use them.

Everett sequestered Anne in the lake house while he figured that one out. The divorce was to be uncontested. I was at loose ends. Ev and Katherine empathized, took me in hand. Katherine really took me in hand, made the first bold move on me, and I didn't hesitate.

To say things had deteriorated on the family front would be quite an understatement. This was in 1963, and the world was crazy, anyway. Vietnam. Marches and protests. Black Panthers. Katherine was forty-four, I was twenty-two. It was all very complicated. Let's just say Katherine and I got together in '63. Victimless crimes are a myth. The degree of victimization was the point. But we lasted for another forty years, Katherine and I.

එඩා

Shortly after the birth, fate put us on a road trip. Everett needed a new special-order Cadillac convertible delivered to Los Angeles and wanted me to drive it there, pick up another car and drive it back. Katherine thought it would be fun to go along. Ev thought that was fine. We could make a vacation of it. Katherine and I felt we'd been granted a genie wish, weeks together, no motel nooners and subsequent anxiety. She was very fond of Everett and so was I.

Our affair had started at the *Carmody Hospital Style Show*, a big charity deal put on every year by the city's cream of society. Katherine was modeling a daring red ball gown, strapless, with a slit up one side that revealed, in a walk, her long legs. She was to be accompanied on the runway by Everett but he refused. Somehow, I got the escort position. I'd been assigned a spot in the show anyway, thanks to Katherine, but a single quick turn on the catwalk in a suit or sport coat, carrying a Burberry overcoat which I was to put on at my turn, walk back. Instead, I was now to escort Katherine while in a tux with a red lining in the coat; open the jacket as she turned, to show the matching color to her gown. I'd never done anything like this before. I had a couple of shots of bourbon before the walk, and, in the dressing room, it was just Katherine and me. She asked me to unzip her gown from behind. "Got to adjust my boobs, honey. The ribbing is killin' 'em."

Somehow, we became rather involved after I unzipped her and she had to apply new makeup at the dressing table. She wiped the lipstick from my face with rough swipes of tissue dipped in creamy makeup remover. "Hold still, dammit. You don't want lipstick all over your face. And see if you can't calm down below the ol' cummerbund, too, honey. That would give the matrons something to talk about." She patted the bulge.

They said we did well and looked good together.

"A little wicked," one of her friends said. "A bit dangerous. Fairly prancing on that runway, you two, very…professional," she said, giving us a long thoughtful look.

∽ↄℰↄ

November was beautiful in Nebraska. If you lived out a ways you heard the distant pops of small gauge shotguns and throatier sounds of the choked twelves. Smelled the leaf fires. Felt the marching drums from football games. Pheasant time. Back then in 1963, there were plenty of birds, but not so many now I heard. The hunters had to go farther, South Dakota, Wyoming. But those days were overlaid with autumn gold and promise and the quickening thrill of winter to come. The blood flowed with a viscosity very nearly perfect, promoting a clarity of vision that was almost psychedelic.

"I doubt we'll be back by Thanksgiving, Ev," she said, kissing him and rubbing his back. Everett said if she wasn't, he'd find a bird to stuff, waggling his eyebrows in mock surprise when I laughed at that. "Hell, take your time, kids, it's been a strange year. We may not even do Christmas this year."

The temptation here was to get all erotic and start detailing things as they happened along the way. Did it in my mind a hundred times. But that would degrade the relationship. It was really quite nice, once you got over the obvious hoodwinking and artifice we had to employ. It was even chaste in some ways. And fun. Katherine had a salty sense of humor and laughed easily.

She could bring me out of my hangover doldrums with a sidelong glance, a dimple deepening just a centimeter. "I'm dry as a nun's, get me a martin-eye, honey" Or after a long session of lovemaking, when offered a cigarette, "Honey, I'm already smokin', singed fringe, know what I mean?"

She made me laugh even when she was in hospice in 2000.

I realized I'd been in love with her since meeting her and since the rush I'd gotten from her to join the family. A shrink might have said I'd transferred that to Anne in the beginning and there might have been some weight to it.

That summer of Anne was a booze-fueled whirl of parties, country-clubbing, meeting people, and it was all intensified because I lived at their house for a month or so. That closeness, the preparation, the chemistry, drew us ever closer.

We submitted. I knew I was in love, I just didn't know who the object of that tempestuous hormonal and wholly irrational cannonade was.

Besides that, I was a lush. So was Katherine. So were we all. But we were a fine-looking bunch for a while.

ᑫᔐᑫᔐ

If Fellini and Tempest Storm had met Masters and Johnson and they'd collaborated on a book, made a film of it with Disney and the Coen Brothers, we'd have been that movie. And a long movie it was. Beginning with the style show and the road trip to California. The journey out was playful, uninhibited, inventive, and joyous.

Our reasoning was that if we overdid it, we'd get it out of our systems and live happily ever after. But I could never get enough of her. She felt the same.

Something about us together made her say, "We'll never be able to stop, will we? This will go on and on."

I shook my head "Yes, I think that's right."

It wasn't a '60s thing, a casual pairing. There were so many of those back then. Beyond the quickening we felt, there was also a deep fondness that would prove to last. I'd admit I was taken by her looks when I first met her. Anne said all of her boyfriends fell for her mom and she hated it.

Katherine's hair glowed. Streaky blonde, always pulled back in a chignon. Pretty face, full lips but not like those pumped up things they did now, ears with diamonds or stones of some kind, sometimes hoops. Darkish eyebrows, long eyelashes. Straight nose line. As I said, a face like Lana Turner, body too. Breasts of any size, small to large, were attractive to me, and hers were large—I'd seen *Tempest Storm's* at The Follies in Kansas City, with some male friends, all of us whooping self-consciously. Katherine was built like that, curvaceous, probably a bit overweight by today's standards, but quite a nice figure for the '60s and well beyond. As late as 1988, she was walking out by where we lived in Maui, and a man drove his car right into a tree ogling her. "I've still got *it*, honey," she told me, and I agreed.

When she put her hair down, it fell below her shoulders and the constant chignon made it curl in a thick tendril which lay across her upper back or her collarbone in front. I'd always thought she would look good with it down or spread across her shoulders, but the way she wore it was *her*, and I liked it pulled back. She wasn't a true blonde; neither was Lana Turner probably, I don't know.

છ્ઝ્છ્

In the Mojave, I turned off at Katherine's request. The euphemism back then was *powder my nose*. The main highway was deserted but she wanted to go on a secondary road to nowhere, so she wouldn't be interrupted. I headed down a packed dirt road that looked solid enough and drove for quite a while.

"I can still see the highway," she said, "so some

trucker could see me squatting like a squaw, honey. Keep going."

I did.

Then the road inexplicably sprouted telephone poles on one side. I remarked on that, and she said, "Phone poles are everywhere, honey. People have to have phones."

I thought it was odd with no sign of a town or even a house Eventually, as the road got worse and the Caddy wallowed along in sand and soft spots, I saw a phone booth. Nothing else. That's where the phone lines stopped, at a phone booth where two dirt roads crossed. Surreal.

I slowed and pulled over just to look at this somewhat disorienting juxtaposition of glass, aluminum frame and desert. And the phone was ringing.

"You get the phone," she said, "This is far enough, I *have* to go." She took her purse and was out of sight on the passenger side, even with the top down. I got out and went to the phone booth. I heard her voice from the other side of the car say, "If it's for me, I'll be right there, honey."

"Hello?" I scanned the bleak landscape, feeling foolish for answering the insistent ring. A small creature moved from one lengthening saguaro cactus shadow to another.

"Where've you been?" a male voice said. He sounded irritated.

"On the way to LA," I said "On the way here, I guess."

"Great. Just fucking great. Well, I need you to go to Vegas. It's all set for Friday. Dallas at noon. You have to be the alibi for Gene. You played poker with him all night Thursday or some shit. Okay?"

"I think you have the wrong person."

There was silence, maybe breathing, and then the phone went dead. I hung it back up. Katherine was in the car doing something to her face in the mirror. Actually powdering her nose.

"Whooee, my eyeteeth were floatin', honey. Who were you talking to?" she asked, when I slid behind the wheel.

"I don't know. Some guy said Friday, noon, Dallas. And I was to be Gene's alibi. In Vegas."

As we turned to head back to the highway, I saw a rooster tail of dust approaching from a side road. A vehicle moving fast for the conditions. I sped up at that point and was quite a ways off when that vehicle came to a complete stop. At the phone booth. The vehicle was an olive drab jeep, but beyond that I couldn't tell much by looking in the rearview mirror. Seemed to be two people in the swirl of dust the jeep raised, but I wasn't sure. When I reached the highway, I floored it and put distance between us and that phone booth. No jeep would ever catch us, and none tried that I could see. It could have been a military vehicle or a surplus military vehicle.

"Are we fleeing? Am I your moll?" Katherine asked, some fifty miles down the road. She was curled up on the seat, back to the window, facing me. Smiling.

I was cruising at eighty now, the heavy Cadillac holding the surface smoothly. I spoke out of the side of my mouth saying "Just like a dame, all the time questions."

She lit a cigarette, then another, and handed me one. I reached over and squeezed her thigh, high under her skirt before I took the cigarette.

"I'll give you twenty minutes to stop that, honey," she said. She said it a lot. It was one of our "things."

ⱸⱭⱸⱭ

It took another hundred miles but I forgot the episode at the phone booth and the military-type jeep, or stashed it well back in my mind behind other things of more timely importance, where to stay the night, where to eat, whether to dress for dinner. Katherine nodded off a couple of times but snapped back awake. I hoped never to see her drool in sleep, but knew it would not diminish my deep affection for her, or the strong attraction. Indeed, we were becoming more and more used to one another's bodies, habits, and humanness that closeness brings with it. Married couples sometimes recoil from something so contrary to the original dream of perfection, and that's the beginning of the end. Couples who embraced the imperfections were the other fifty percent in my opinion. I loved Katherine, all of her.

November in the Mojave was nowhere near the storied heat of summer, although it could get up around ninety degrees. It was about seventy when Katherine and I blew through. We left the top down a lot so we could see everything, red tailed hawks floating here and there, little sand devils, Joshua trees and countryside. We did pull over and raise the top when the wind blew grit into the car. We kissed and made out like a couple of highschoolers, turned on the air-conditioner, smoked, and talked while we finished the final two canned Manhattans swimming in the cold water and ice left in the cooler. Not advisable in the desert, by the way, but we were almost out of the Mojave.

"What do you think that phone call was about?" she asked.

"Wrong number? I don't know. Unless it was a right number and the guy didn't get there in time. In that case, it's a little scary. Friday, Dallas, your favorite president is there. God knows why," I said.

"Oh, campaigning I imagine. With that troll Johnson. Who knows? Anyway, I just think he's kind of sexy."

"Sexier than me?" I pulled her toward me and kissed her.

"I'll give you twenty minutes to stop that, honey," she said, between kisses, and squeezed me strategically.

We tasted like Manhattans and cigarettes and our lips

were cold from the drinks. We were dusty. Our clothing was wrinkled. We were happy. Completely.

❧❧❧

The motel was nice, seemed fairly new, and big. Back then motels were pretty easy choices, the seedy ones were missing neon letters and the really bad ones had little shotgun cottages scattered about, or sad teepee-shaped structures out this way. The new ones were built on the order of hotels with elevators and fountains in the lobby, lots of glass and lights.

This one said *Four Stars* under the main sign, and it gleamed in the gently descending dusk as we drove up under the portals to the entrance. A bellhop opened Katherine's door, and pushed a chrome luggage cart around to the trunk. At the desk, the attractive receptionist asked, "Will you and your…will you all be staying with us for one night or more, Mr. Waller?"

It turned out they were almost fully booked, and so instead of two separate rooms, she asked if we would mind a suite for a reduced price. I said fine, and we were on our way, bellhop in tow.

We unpacked and took a shower—"Come on in, honey. We're still in the desert so we'd better conserve water."—and dressed casually. We headed downstairs to the tiki-themed bar, empty at this hour. The bartender, a large man with a graying crewcut, about forty-years-of-age, in an Aloha shirt, raised his head slightly. It was an inquisitive look, which he abruptly shed, smiling, placing coasters in front of us.

Katherine looked at me, said, "Want to try a Honi-Honi, honey?"

"Trader Vic's, right? Which one?" said the bartender.

"Beverly Hills Hilton," she said, tapping a cigarette on her gold case.

The bartender and I produced lighters. He won. She took a drag, raised her head, showing her long tanned neck, and blew the smoke above us. The bartender was entranced. She flicked ash into the ashtray he slid toward her. I was used to men honing in on Katherine and no longer frightened by it. Is frightened an odd word? Frightened of what? Of loss? Of physical entanglement with the more aggressive types? No. Of unpleasantness touching our charmed existence, I suppose. She handled it well, having been exposed to it most of her life.

"I hate to be inquisitive, but what are you doing here—well, that's none of my business. How about just an annoying question? Like, could I have your autograph?"

He clicked a ballpoint, tore a sheet of paper from an order pad, and offered them to Katherine.

She smiled. I watched her write *Two Honi-Honie's, pronto. K. Riley,* a flourish on the Y. She handed it back to him.

He read it, laughed. "Coming right up, but only if

you sign your real name, Ms. Turner." He waited. "Come on, I'm a fan. Sign it to Rocco."

She signed the same slip of paper with *AKA Lana Turner, to Rocco*, and added a heart. He put the slip in his Aloha shirt pocket and whirled about to make our drinks.

"So who am I?" I said.

"Johhny Stompanato's successor. Better treat me right."

"I intend to."

♥♥♥

Word got around that the guests in the yellow Cadillac with Nebraska dealer plates were Lana Turner and some younger guy. We decided to move on the next day, but first we'd play with the attention and have fun with it. We walked outside before dinner and smoked, watching a harvest moon come up large.

"Drop the mask, honey," she said.

"What, the movie star mix-up?"

"No that's just some fun stuff. Your mask. Your being 'on' all the time. You don't need it."

"I'm not sure I—"

"Don't play dumb, Les. I love you to death. You, the real you."

"And I am fucking crazy about you, always will be."

"Love me, love my bunions."

"What?"

"In twenty years I'll be sixty-four. You'll be forty-four. Get it? Saggy boobs, cellulite, and stuff I don't even want to think about. At eighty-four, you'll be sixty-four."

"Sure. I don't care. It's you for me. Somehow, I don't know how. There are...obstacles. But it's you, Katherine."

"Okay. Let's do room service tonight, blow this pop-stand in the morning."

"Perfect."

"I won't leave Everett. And I don't want to ever hurt him."

❧❧❧

We had prime ribs, a bottle of good wine, and walked on the adjoining golf course in the moonlight. Katherine carried her shoes, enjoying the fresh dew on the cut grass. I carried the bottle and the wine glasses. Neither of us sensed a thing. Creatures sense impending earthquakes, horses see ghosts, and dogs know evil when it seeps into their space. We were clueless in our short-sightedness.

Friday morning, the sun woke us, the curtains open on our second-floor suite. Palm trees, mountains, clear sky. Over brunch we checked the AAA maps and decided on a leisurely last leg into LA. The TV was on, some soap opera murmuring.

Katherine did face things with creams in the bathroom, the door open, leaning at the mirror over the sink.

In the next few moments, the world changed, the axis shifted, but this time I sensed it before the news bulletin broke in. The president had been shot. I looked at my watch. 10:40. It would be 12:40 in Dallas. The bulletin came from New York. "Bulletin, 12:40 p.m., in Dallas, Texas, three shots were fired at President Kennedy's motorcade. The first reports say the President was seriously wounded, that he slumped over in Mrs. Kennedy's lap, she cried out, 'Oh, no!' and the motorcade went on...The wounds perhaps could be fatal..."

I put my coffee down, glanced at Katherine, still busy at the mirror, something caught in my throat, acid-like. The Mojave phone call went through my mind. The phone rang in the suite. It rang five or six times and stopped. I stood transfixed. Katherine was near, I smelled her perfume, heard her moving.

"The phone," she said. "Oh my god. Something's wrong. Is it Everett?" I looked at the phone on the end table, a red light was flashing. I see it in my dreams sometimes. The bulletin about Dallas continued.

I picked up the phone. It was a message from the desk. I returned the call, but there was no answer for several rings. Then finally a breathless voice said, "Hello? I mean Front Desk, yes?"

"This is Room 216. The message light was on?"

"Oh yes. Yes. There was an emergency call from Omaha for Mrs. Riley. Mr. Riley was taken to the emergency room this morning. She is to call a Mrs. Bickle at this number—do you have a pen?"

I wrote the number down. Fran Bickle was a family friend. I gave it to Katherine and walked in a daze back to the television. Kennedy was in grave condition, they seemed to be saying. Shot from a park or a building. Then I heard Katherine's voice, "Oh no. Oh my god, Fran, what?" Then silence. "Fran, I'll call you back. It's not your fault, hon."

I waited.

"It's Ev. He had a heart attack," Katherine said.

"Will he recover?" I gestured at the TV. "Was it this?"

"No, honey. He died this morning."

She sat heavily on the couch, and I held her. I felt her body shake from crying. I was numb, it seemed. The voice from the TV droned on. Katherine's quakes slowed, and then stopped.

"What was Fran doing there so early?" she said, muffled by my shoulder.

"Maybe checking on him? Stopped by for some reason?"

"I should talk," she said.

Some talking head, Cronkite I guess, made the pious most of his moment of national grief. Others would follow. The Dan Rathers believed they framed the thoughts for us poor dumb clucks, leaderless now except for Uncle Cornpone.

What a time. My core ached for Katherine and the people around JFK.

C/OC/O

I took Katherine to the new Los Angeles airport, and the Caddy to the dealership. I drove the exchange car, alone, through the Mojave and on Route 66. I guess I stopped to sleep. I must have. I drove on to Omaha for the funeral.

After the funeral, Anne and Teddy's kid, Longworth as Anne called him now, Katherine, and I flew to Maui and stayed at the new Sheraton for a couple of weeks. We frequented bookshops, stores, spent time at the pool and the beach. We were sleepwalking through life for a while, all of us, except Longworth. He enjoyed Maui immensely.

I met Teddy at the little airport. He was hesitant, walking toward me from the little needle-nosed plane from the big island, but I hugged him. We resumed our old college friendship.

He and Anne went off to see the waterfalls of Hana, taking little Longworth with them. Katherine and I were left to ourselves. We didn't take up where we left off; at least not for some days. We did enjoy one another, our company, and the odd moments of laughter. Life went on.

C/OC/O

My own family hadn't disowned me, but they were distant. The affair with Katherine was not to their liking. They thought it would blow over.

Katherine was quite wealthy by then, and Anne was well-fixed and married to Teddy. I was odd man out, financially and, though it never would have been an issue with Katherine, I wouldn't be kept.

So I took steps to become financially viable. I borrowed $30,000 and went to Hollywood with a screenplay. That worked out well, with the Los Cruiseros biker gang series and the rest was history. I was never quite as bankable as Katherine but I could hold up my end, and did. She was proud of me. We lived well and happily for years.

❦❦❦

Something odd from that time: the LA Cadillac dealer said some military intelligence sorts were snooping about, trying to discern who had driven the car from Omaha.

The dealer told them there were no records of the cross-country drivers. He told them to check with the Omaha dealership. They did and were told the same—no records had been kept of the drivers. The car had been delivered and that was that.

❦❦❦

Katherine was lucid and sharp to the very end. In 2000, she was diagnosed with incurable cancer. Her health failed but not her mind. "Honey, I'm gonna smoke and drink right up to the end. Get me a martin-eye."

They said she could undergo chemo and radiation therapy, but for what? A few months more to live, and painful ones at that?

She was in relatively little pain, and with meds, even less.

"Remember the phone call?" she said one day, out of the blue. "The Mojave call?"

"I do, indeed."

"I believe that call set off the happiest days of my life, and the worst."

"Best of times, worst of times," I said.

"Don't get all literary on my lame ass, honey." Then she laughed.

છ૭છ૭

I made some inquiries. The phone booth was still there, but the company was going to shut it down that year, remove it. I'd have to move fast.

છ૭છ૭

Teddy and Anne flew in. Longworth was now thirty-seven, and a lawyer. He was there with his wife and kids.

Some of the Omaha old guard were there. Some had younger wives. In the parking lot of the hospice the set-builders had been thorough: sand, saguaro cactus, tumbleweeds, the phone booth with all its forty years of graffiti and sandstorm-dimmed glass. Next to it all was a showroom mint yellow 1964 Cadillac convertible.

They brought her out in her wheelchair. Wheeled her to the phone booth. The phone was ringing. I poured her a martini.

She took a sip. "You answer it, honey. Tell me if it's for me."

OLD ORDNANCE

Crates. I'm hopeful that for my trouble, one arm tourniqueted with baling twine and useless for now, that they contain something wondrous, like RPGs or, at least AKs, something the psychos in ski masks would buy, pay big money for.

I pry-bar one open, one-handed. Then another. But they all contain early M-14s, useless fuckers. Everyone knew they jammed, but then the conditions in desert country were so different than in Vietnam. At least the humidity wouldn't be what shut them off in mid-burst.

Brand new, packed in cosmoline all these years. Ten to a crate. Where'd they come from? Kennedy was alive and banging Marilyn Monroe when these things were assembled. Willmarth had just said ordnance, crates of it.

They *look* cool. Like in that old photo op for Kerry back then, flak jacket, helmet straps hanging unbuckled. Run for president stuff. Except Clinton and Bush both sidestepped the shit, became president without the cool photo. Dodged all the bullets. And Obama. What a laugh. Fuck 'em all but eight, six to carry you, two to pull the wagon, as my old man used to say.

If Willmarth sells these antiques to the camel-fuckers, it's no more a crime than Holder running guns to the cartels. If they buy them. Maybe they're not quite that dumb. Then I'm stuck with twenty-two crates of worthless fullies that a good sandstorm will make into fine doorstops.

My arm hurts. Slug must've hit a bone before it exited. I can work for hours with one arm, loading these crates on a flatbed trailer, cover them with hay bales. If I don't pass out. But I don't have hours. Or I can just leave them for the rednecks who probably thought they'd won the Kansas lottery. This was to be my score. I'm too old for this shit. Who tipped those shit-kickers off?

Those guys in the platform pickups'll be back. And they'll bring the hoo-raw boys with them. I don't think I killed anyone, but one of the trucks drove off on a rim throwing sparks, and the back windows imploded on both vehicles when I fired left-handed. But they kept going.

They have cellphones. I don't have time. If I had two good arms, I could load these fuckers. I can hear my old man, "If a frog had wings, he wouldn't bump his ass a'hoppin. Get the hell outa here while you can."

The ER will call a cop if I just walk in. I'll call Willmarth. He's got a vet who works quiet for cash. Shit, just shoot me. I'm out the crates, have to hide my truck, leave the trailer, pay the vet for a patchup. I could cry. This was gonna be my trip to Mexico, live like a king. If the arm's too fucked up, I'll have to get it fixed. Medicare's gonna love that.

Oh shit, headlights. Oh, bigger shit, red and blue flashers.

The car's lights follow the ground, disappearing in the slight draws, aiming at the sky as it crests the hillocks. Then it's on me. I'm dizzy, maybe loss of blood. I'm looking at free meals the rest of my life. Prison doc will patch me up good, if he's not a hack. Never thought it would end this way. If only I had come earlier. My old man chimes in again. "Junior, if ifs and buts were candy and nuts, we'd all have a merry Christmas."

The spotlight is on me. I lace my fingers on my head. The pain ratchets up in my right arm, oh God. A voice says, "What's up, Junior?"

I know this cop. It's RC. We were drafted about the same time way back then. I knew he was county now but only had a beer with him once. It's not like we're buddies. He's past retirement age.

"What you got in there, Junior?" he asks again.

"Twenty-two cases M-14s."

"M-14s. Antiques. Where'd they come from?"

"No idea. Some armory but back in the day. Untraceable."

"You got a buyer?"

"Guy in Texas. Unless he don't want 14s."

"Naw, 14s'll sell." Then he laughed. "The Nichols boys are scared shitless, said there was an army out here, a militia that fired on them. They was out here looking to steal a four-wheeler. Admitted it. Said they fired back with .22s but was outmanned, outgunned. They didn't say anything about crates."

"Now what?"

"Were you working this alone?"

"That was my plan," I said.

"Change it." He looks at me with no expression, hand resting on his holstered gun butt. Just a place to keep his hand, though. I can tell it's not threatening. Snap's still shut.

"Okay."

"Now, let's get you to a doc with this accidental self-inflicted gunshot wound."

"What about the Nicholses?"

"In the cooler for the night. Drunk and baked both. When we come back here, you can watch me load that trailer."

"I figure hay bales on it and down to McAllen, Texas," I say.

"Sounds good. Get in."

"Crates be okay?"

"Owner's gone, asked me to look in now and then. They'll be fine as frog's hair."

"You talk like my old man," I say and get in.

At the ER, they said, "Lucky it was a .22. Just nicked a bone, arteries okay."

RC turns the cop car in, end of shift, and we take his truck back out there with a twelve-pack. I call Willmarth. He says 14s are fine. He says, "Hell I could move Red Ryders with plastic stocks. Bring it."

JOHN SETTLE

Eighty-seven. Full life, they'll say. Full, anyway, of something. Settle came to California in 1935. *Propelled by dust storms like great roiling theater curtains, bulldozed shotgun shack, shared cotton crop zeroed out.*

Now California was trying to be Kansas eighty years later. To dust.

Thought it was the green and promised land. Seen so much.

Shuffle-stepped, soft-shoed humming, singing, "Getcher kicks. On Route Sixty-Six."

He had.

Kicks to the head as a seven-year old.

Khaki-clad men, crop cops for the landowners, his mother going with a pair of them at night.

Goddamn why would you think of that? Migrant whore, they said.

Spat it, didn't just say it.

Fear. Hate. Pain. Rage. "Don't forget, Wy-nona, San Bernadeeno, kicks, ever plan to motor west."

Hummed it, little jump step. His knee hurt.

"Hell to get old," he said to the dog that watched him. "But you know that."

The dog's tail moved once. He thumped over on his side, exhaled, closed his cloudy eyes and slept.

Early on, the scene, man. Seemed right, seemed cool. Got high. Read a lot. Jack, Howl, Bill, Road, Steinbeck stuck with him but a 1930s copy of Napoleon Hill in tatters thrust him forward, shot him at the moon. He shed the jungled friends.

Jobs. Warehouses. Bridges. Boomtime. Scraping. Saving.

Settle Inn Motels, all over the west, the dream. Three of them the reality.

Torrance, Culver City, San Pedro.

Prosperous, then not.

Fling with Vegas in the fifties. Part owner Cactus Flower Casino. Kicked out by eye-ties, the mean-eyed Jew, muttering through cigars.

Had the knack for a few years, lost it.

John Stark Settle. Back to the wall.

Splash. Ol' Kentuck into the glass, two fingers. Cheap. Burning.

Drink from a glass, not the bottle, and you're not a shitbum.

A clean glass.

Weighed the cold Smith and Wesson 357, released the cylinder to gravity, checked the loads—.38 pluses. Hollowpoints.

Solid gun. A Burroughs piece.

Snap the cylinder shut, click like an old Cadillac door. Pink convertible.

The dog's front feet moved. Chasing something in a dream, Settle thought. I was always doing that.

Damn near caught it, too.

One stored number on the cellphone. "Come pick up the dog tonight," to Marie's voicemail. She had dogs, a little land. "I'm going back to Kansas."

Closed the door softly behind him.

Walked to the empty ruined pool, climbed down the chromed ladder. He'd sold this motel thirty years before. To be demolished next month. The sign said a health clinic. Coming soon.

He remembered the chromed ladder and how much it had cost. Blisters of rust scraped his hands as he descended.

Expensive chromed steel. Custom made.

Made irrelevant.

The pocked and gray and spray-graffitied pool wall obscured all but some of the faded steel turquoise sign from where he stood in the leaves and trash.

Amoeba-shaped they'd called it. The sign. When bright.

Settle Inn. *For the Best Rest in the West*, said a smaller sign. Beneath it.

About the Author

Guinotte Wise has been a creative director in advertising most of his working life. In his youth he put forth effort as a bull rider, ironworker, laborer, funeral home pickup person, bartender, truck driver, postal worker, ice house worker, and paving field engineer. A staid museum director called him raffish, which he enthusiastically embraced—the observation, not the director. Of course, he took up writing fiction and poetry.

Wise welds and writes on a farm in Resume Speed, KS. His first collection of short stories, *Night Train, Cold Beer*, won the H. Palmer Hall Award for short fiction. His novel, *Ruined Days*, and his anthology, *Resume Speed*, are available at Amazon, Barnes & Noble, Kobo and wherever fine books are sold. His work has been seen in over forty literary reviews and anthologies, including *Atticus*, *Thrice Fiction*, and *The MacGuffin*. More of his work may be seen at http://www.wisesculpture.com His wife has an honest job in the city and drives 100 miles a day to keep it.